A NOTE TO READERS

While the Brannon and Harvey families are fictional, the situations they faced in Cincinnati during the Civil War are very real. Famous people as well as ordinary soldiers and civilians wrote diaries, letters, and memoirs that give us a great deal of information about life during the four-year war. Food was often in short supply, and widows and their children had to depend on help from others to survive.

In northern states like Ohio, feelings against the "Rebels," as Southern soldiers were called, ran high. Like Milt Finney, some people in the North had sons who chose to fight for the South. They faced prejudice every day.

By the end of the war, people in both the North and South were bitter about the suffering they had experienced. Most historians believe that President Lincoln had the best chance of bringing forgiveness between the North and the South when peace was declared. Because of his assassination, we will never know if the hard times people in the South experienced after the war could have been avoided.

J
F
Sis

SISTERS IN TIME

Elise

the Actress

CLIMAX OF THE CIVIL WAR

NORMA JEAN LUTZ

BARBOUR
PUBLISHING

Elise

the Actress

Cover design by Lookout Design Group, Inc.

Published by Barbour Publishing, Inc., P.O. Box 719, Uhrichsville, Ohio 44683 www.barbourbooks.com

Our mission is to publish and distribute inspirational products offering exceptional value and biblical encouragement to the masses.

 Member of the
Evangelical Christian
Publishers Association

Printed in the United States of America.
5 4 3 2 1

CONTENTS

CHAPTER 1

New Year's Eve

Music and laughter floated throughout the expanse of the large Brannon house. The guests who'd come for the New Year's Eve celebration were dancing and singing and visiting. If Elise Brannon stood still and closed her eyes, she could almost forget for a moment that a war existed. The War Between the States was now going into its fourth long year.

But at this moment, she had no time to close her eyes because there was too much to do. Elise and her friend Verly Boyd were in the kitchen just off the ballroom. Berdeen O'Banion, their Irish maid and nanny, expected both Elise and Verly to help take the large serving trays full of food and pass them among the guests.

Handing a tray to Verly, Elise said, "Can you handle this one? It's pretty heavy."

Verly's blue eyes shone as she smiled. "I can handle it just fine."

Elise picked up another tray and said, "Forward, march. I'm right behind you."

"Careful you'll be, lassies," Berdeen said as she held open the door that led from the large kitchen into a pass-through and out into the formal ballroom.

Before the war, Mama would have hired extra help for such an occasion, but Elise didn't mind helping at all. In fact, she rather enjoyed it.

As she moved among the crowd, she heard her papa saying, "I never thought I'd live to see the day—Congress finally allowing the contrabands to fight in their own war for freedom."

"And good soldiers they've made, I hear," another man put in.

To which Elise's papa retorted, "I've been trying to tell people that for many years. Now they can see it for themselves—clear as day."

Elise knew that contraband referred to the freed slaves. Ever since President Lincoln had issued the Emancipation Proclamation a year ago, freed slaves had been longing to don uniforms and join the fighting. At last it had happened. Elise's papa, Attorney Jack Brannon, had long been a fighter for the abolition of slavery. Elise was overjoyed that his dreams were at last coming true.

As Elise moved through the little knots of people gathered in the vast ballroom, she also heard men discussing President Lincoln's speech at the battleground in Gettysburg last November. Others discussed the ineptness of Union generals. Conversation of the women covered men who were off in battle and the work being done at various hospitals to aid the war wounded.

Verly's papa had died in the first fighting at Bull Run, and now her brother, Alexander, was off fighting, as well. She and her mother had been forced to sell their home and move into Aunt Ella's boardinghouse. Mrs. Boyd supplemented their meager income by taking in sewing. All these troubles had made Verly understandably sad.

Through the crowd, Elise could see her friend smiling shyly as she offered her tray of sandwiches to the guests. At least the festivities had managed to cheer Verly and keep her smiling.

After her tray of meat and cheese was emptied, Elise went over to Verly. "It's time to gather our troupe and go to the playroom," she said.

"Oh, good!" Verly's eyes lit up. "This'll be such fun!"

After taking their trays back to the kitchen, Elise said, "We're going to the playroom now, Berdeen. Will you come and help?"

"Aye, lassie. I mun put the fresh teakettle back on the stove, and I'll be with ye."

"Verly, you go gather the others. Berdeen and I'll go up the back way. We'll meet you upstairs."

Verly gave a little giggle. "Meet you upstairs."

A few moments later, Elise entered the playroom, where her brothers and the other children of attending guests were gathered. From the table, she picked up Mama's little portable writing desk.

"Make a straight line," she said, making checks on the paper lying atop the wooden frame she was holding. "Let's have the old-est at this end, down to the youngest." She watched as they scram-bled a moment to line up, some having to ask the age of the others.

"But I don't want to be on the very end," protested Elise's eight-year-old brother, Peter. "I always have to be on the tail end."

"It doesn't mean anything bad, Peter," Elise said in a gentle tone. "It simply serves to make our presentation more organized." She took him by the arm and guided him to the end of the line.

"I don't mind being on the end," Verly said. "I'll trade places."

"Hurrah for Verly," Peter said. "Let's trade."

But Elise shook her head. "It's important that one person be the organizer, Peter. Stay where you're placed."

Peter groaned, and Verly reached out to pat his arm in sympathy.

Just then Berdeen, who was keeping watch in the hallway, stuck her head in the door. "Be ye nigh ready?"

Berdeen had promised she would help get the adults seated and quiet just before Elise and her troupe were ready to come downstairs to perform their recitations.

"A few more minutes, Berdeen," Elise said.

Elise hoped that the humorous recitations she'd chosen would brighten the evening for everyone. The other youngsters were agreeable. Earlier in the evening, they'd all been given scripts and poems to present, and each had had a chance to practice. Now the room fairly bristled with excitement. Even Elise's older brother, Samuel, had acquiesced to her leadership—which was a surprise. At eleven, a full year older than Elise, Samuel could be pretty bossy at times. But as he said, this program was all her idea. Because Samuel followed, the other two older boys, Cleve and Adam Scott, did the same. The Kilgour sisters were also cooperative. With a little luck, Elise's plan would come off smooth as silk.

"Let's run through the order of presentations one more time," she said, making little checks on her list as she did so. Once she was satisfied that each one knew his or her place and lines, she said to Samuel, "Tell Berdeen we're ready."

Samuel strode to the door, opened it, and gave Berdeen a wave.

"Stay at the balcony rail and watch," she told Samuel, "then let us know when they're ready."

It took a few minutes for Berdeen to quiet the revelers and get them all into the parlor and seated. When it was time, Elise led her troupe to the balcony. At her signal, the first half of the line went down one of the curving twin staircases while the last half took the other. They converged at the bottom, fell back into line, and marched into the parlor, where the gathered guests applauded their entrance.

Reading from her written notes, Elise introduced her troupe and then announced the first presentation. "Each member of our troupe will recite a verse from a humorous poem titled, 'Our Minister's Sermon.'"

Sandy-haired Cleve Scott stepped forward. He was a bit nervous at having to go first, but as the oldest of their little conclave, he wanted to set a good example. Clearing his throat, he gave the opening lines.

Elise smiled as twitters and chuckles swept over the crowd. Next it was Adam's turn with the second verse:

I tell you our minister's prime; he is—
But I couldn't quite determine,
When I heard him givin' it right and left,
Just who was hit by his sermon.
Of course, there couldn't be no mistake
When he talked about long-winded prayin'
For Peters and Johnson, they sot and scowled
At ev'ry word he wuz sayin'.

Following Adam, Samuel took his turn speaking clear and full as though he were already a professional attorney like his papa. Amelia and Madeline Kilgour took the next two verses.

Elise scanned the crowd and saw the smiles on the faces. Her heart raced. There was Aunt Ella, whose husband, Dr. George Harvey, was off tending wounded soldiers at the front lines. Beside her sat her elder daughter, Melissa Baird, whose husband, Jeremiah, was also in the war. Alicia and Alan, the Harveys' fifteen-year-old twins, were too old to be a part of this troupe, but they were both laughing aloud at the skit.

It was fairly possible that at this time next year Alan might be in the heat of battle, as well. Elise knew he was torn between staying home to care for his mother and sisters or answering his call to duty.

Elise's papa was smiling, as were his business associates. Mama was standing in the doorway beside Berdeen, and Mama's beautiful dark eyes were crinkling with laughter. How thankful Mama was that Papa was past the age of serving in the war—how thankful they all were.

Now Verly stepped forward. Though her voice was rather soft, she managed to recite the sixth verse without a mistake. When she was done, the laughter in the room had grown a bit more boisterous. Peter, loving the sound of it, launched into his part:

Just then the minister sez, sez he,
"And now I've come to the fellers
Who've lost this shower by usin' their friends
As a sort of moral umbrellers.
Go home!" sez he, "and find your faults
Instead of huntin' your brother's.
Go home," sez he, "and wear the coats
You're trying to fit on others!"

Elise had to wait a moment for the laughter to subside before she finished with the final verse:

My wife she nudged, and Brown he winked,
And there wuz lots of smilin',
And lots of lookin' at our pew—
It sot my blood a-bilin'.
Sez I to myself, "Our minister
Is gettin' a little bitter,
I'll tell him when the meetin's out
That I ain't that kind of a critter."

At Elise's hand motion, her cast made their bows and curtsies to the sound of rousing applause. Then the Kilgour sisters went to the piano and played a duet while the others sang about a fly on the head of a bald-headed man.

Following the song, which also caused a good deal of guffaws and snickers, each performer gave a short recitation, beginning with Peter. Elise stood back near the piano with her notes as each of the troupe members performed.

The grand finale was to be a recitation titled "How We Hunted a Mouse," which dramatically told of a husband rushing to the aid of his wife, who was frightened by a mouse. He was rewarded for his efforts by having the mouse crawl up the leg of his trousers. It was Elise's favorite recitation, and she'd liked to have presented it herself, but she deferred the honor to her older brother.

She had laboriously copied it from the recitation book and made it large so it would be easy for Samuel to read. He'd run through it earlier in the playroom and had put all the other children in stitches.

Now she introduced her brother to the crowd. He'd asked her if he could announce his selection himself, and she'd agreed. Samuel stepped forward, and everyone grew quiet. "Our Flag," he said solemnly, "an essay by A. L. Stone."

From behind the piano, Elise tried in vain to get his attention, shaking her head and waving, but he ignored her. Samuel was taking matters into his own hands, after all.

"Ringed about with flame and smoke of rebel batteries," he began, "one solitary flag went down, torn and scathed, on the blackened and battered walls of Sumter."

Inwardly, Elise groaned. The last thing she wanted was for the war to be brought into this happy moment. The whole point of the entertainment was to help the guests forget the war for a little while. Samuel continued:

"Then the slumberous fire burst forth and blazed up from the hearts of the people. The painted symbol of the national life, under which our populations of city and country had walked to and fro with tranquil footstep, stirring its peaceful folds with no shouts of chivalrous and romantic deference, had been torn down and trodden under the feet of traitors."

The Union officers in the room who were in uniform stood to their feet. Samuel held his head high and continued the reading that he'd memorized many months ago.

"It was torn down from a single flagstaff, and as the tidings of that outrage swept, ringing and thrilling through the land, ten thousand banners were run up on every hilltop and in every vale, on church towers and armed fortress and peaceful private homes, till the heavens over us looked down upon more stars than they kept in their own nightly vault. . . ."

Now the rest of the guests were standing. Some held their hands over their hearts in a proud salute. Samuel's eyes were shining.

"And then the cry went forth, 'Rally round the flag, boys!' and every instrument of martial music took up the strain and church bells pealed it forth, and church choirs sang it. . . ."

Elise looked at Mama. Her fair cheeks were wet with tears as were Aunt Ella's and Cousin Melissa's. The men were solemn and grim-faced. That Samuel—why did she agree to let him take the final act?

"And the voices gathered into a mighty chorus that swept over the New England hills and across the breadth of midland prairies and dashed its waves over the summits of the mountains and down these western slopes till they met and mingled with the waves of the Pacific—the full unison echoing here through all our streets and homes, 'Rally round the flag, boys! Rally once again!'"

When he was finished, Samuel bowed his head. It was quiet for a moment, then the entire room erupted into cheers and shouts. "Rally round the flag," some guests called out. "Let this year bring the end to the war!" others cried. "Hurrah for the Union!"

Verly evidently noticed Elise's downcast expression. She came over and put her arm around Elise's shoulder. Ever since Verly and her mother had moved into Aunt Ella's boardinghouse, Verly and Elise had become close friends. Now she seemed to sense how Elise was feeling. "Everyone thinks you planned the program to end like this," she said. "You look like a heroine."

Elise just shook her head. "Oh, Verly, I wanted everyone to laugh and be happy. Laughter is the best medicine. Why can't people forget the terrible war, even if it's only for one evening?"

CHAPTER 2

Sledding

Though Elise was upset with Samuel, it was too nice a party to let a little thing ruin it. Mama had planned to send Peter to bed after the recitations. After all, before Elise turned ten, she was made to go to bed before midnight. But Peter begged so hard that Mama relented.

At the stroke of midnight, Papa partially opened the windows so they could hear the church bells sounding across the city from their vantage point in Walnut Hills. The guests were still somber from Samuel's dramatic reading as they lifted cups of eggnog and punch in toasts to the year of 1864. The long, costly war put a damper on looking forward to a new year. Everyone said it would only be more of the same. Elise wasn't sure she could bear another year of the news of so much killing, so much pain, so much sorrow.

She stared at one of the opened windows as silvery snowflakes came blowing inside. She knew her uncle George was on the battleground in the cold somewhere in Tennessee. And Melissa's husband, Jeremiah, was out in the winter cold somewhere in Virginia. Verly, who was standing close beside her, was quiet. She was no doubt thinking of her slain father and her absent brother.

Papa came to the center of the room and asked that everyone be quiet for a moment. Pastor Terrence Thomas and his wife, Hope, were among the guests, and Papa asked the pastor to pray.

As the guests bowed their heads, Pastor Thomas prayed for an end to the war and violence, for the Union to be preserved, and for family members to be kept safe.

Elise allowed herself a peek at her handsome father as he bowed in prayer. She was terribly proud of him. He was a good and fair attorney and had helped many people by giving his services away. Elise had asked Papa many times why God would allow such a terrible war. He spoke often of the unimaginable atrocities of slavery. "Perhaps," he told her once, "we are suffering God's wrath and judgment for those despicable sins."

Before the war, Elise's papa and another Cincinnati lawyer, Salmon Chase, defended runaway slaves who had no money to defend themselves. Papa still kept in close touch with Mr. Chase, who was now the Secretary of the Treasury in Washington, D.C. Papa knew many people in high places of government. Even though Elise was proud of her father, she couldn't help wishing he had a little more time for her. He was a terribly busy man.

As the prayer continued, Elise heard a little sniff beside her and realized Verly was fighting back her tears. She reached out and took her friend's hand. Verly looked over at Elise and managed a weak smile.

Elise was glad she could be Verly's friend. The Boyds had lost so much since the war began. In spite of Mrs. Boyd's talents as an excellent seamstress, it was a struggle for the two of them. Due to the war, there was so little cloth to be had and so few people were purchasing new clothes. Much of her work was patching, hemming, and altering.

As soon as Pastor Thomas said "amen," someone muttered, "Close those windows, I'm freezing." A ripple of laughter moved through the room, dispelling the solemn mood.

Elise guided Verly closer to the heating stove. "Can you come over tomorrow to play?"

"Mama needs my help in the morning. I may be able to come later."

Elise couldn't imagine having to work during Christmas vacation from school. She was relieved there were no studies to tend to. "When you come, we'll have Berdeen serve us tea up in the playroom. I'll have the dolls ready for a tea party."

Verly's face lit up. "That sounds like such fun. I hope I can come."

The menfolk were pulling on their cloaks and going outside to bring their carriages up to the front portico. There the ladies were able to embark without getting in too much of the deep snow. In spite of having boots, no one liked to get their long skirts wet.

Presently Cousin Alan drove up in the Harvey buggy, and Verly boarded it along with her mother and the Harvey family. Elise waved as her friend departed. Elise hoped the bright evening had helped Verly during this trying time.

Snow continued to fall during the night, and by morning the view outside Elise's upstairs window was of a vast white blanket as far as the eye could see. Down the tree-studded hillside, every bare limb appeared to be coated in creamy white icing, and every house was topped with a dollop of whipped cream. In spite of the chill in the air, she slipped out from beneath the heavy feather comforter, grabbed her wrapper, and stole across the cold floor to the window for a better view.

Just then, Peter came running into her room without even knocking. He was at her side in a flash, fairly exploding with excitement. "Look how deep, Elise. Just look how deep it is. This is the most snow we've had all winter. And on a day with no school!"

"It's beautiful, isn't it?"

"Do you suppose Samuel would go sledding?"

"I suppose you might ask," Elise said.

"You go ask with me."

"You saw last night how well Samuel listens to me," she said, still thinking about how her older brother had changed the closing recitation. "But let's get dressed and eat breakfast. Then we'll see what the day holds."

Elise wanted to remind Peter that *she* could easily go sledding with him, but she knew he put great stock in being included in Samuel's comings and goings. Samuel spent much time talking with Papa about legal matters, war matters, and whatever other matters he felt Papa might want to talk about. Often he worked at the law office doing odd jobs as a clerk and messenger. It was a rare day when Peter could actually play with his older brother.

"Bet I can beat you down to breakfast," Peter said.

"Of course you can, silly." Elise lifted a lock of her long black hair. "You don't have all this to brush and braid."

"Well, I bet I can beat you in a snowball fight."

"That wager I'll accept."

Satisfied, her little brother went bouncing back out of her room. As she turned back to the window, she saw Chancy Wilmot ride up to the Brannon stable on his spotted pony.

At age sixteen, Chancy was old enough to be off fighting, but because he'd had a lame ankle since birth, he was rejected. Papa then hired him to help with the horses. Chancy was quiet and kept to himself, and Papa was pleased at how well he could handle the foals—he was an excellent trainer. Even though they had fewer horses than Elise could ever remember, still there was too much for

Papa to do, even with Samuel's help.

Elise hurried to pull on her day dress and to plait her hair in two long braids. When she arrived in the dining room, Berdeen was already bringing platters of ham and eggs out from the kitchen. Peter was at the table and made a funny face at her. Papa and Samuel were discussing war matters, and Mama listened quietly as she always did.

Midway through breakfast, Elise turned to Peter and said, "Are we still going to go sledding together after we eat?" She gave a secret wink as she said it.

Peter caught on quickly. "We're going sledding, all right. Down the east ridge, and we'll have a swell time."

Samuel spoke up then. "Hey, isn't anyone inviting me to go along?"

Elise smiled at Peter. Her little ploy had worked. To Samuel, she said, "I didn't think you needed an invitation. We assumed you'd want to come, too."

Peter jumped up from his place. "I'll go on out and get the sled down and wax the runners."

"Not so fast," Mama protested. "You've not eaten much breakfast."

But Papa said, "Oh, Louisa, can't you see how excited he is? Let him go. He'll be starved by ten o'clock."

"Thank you, Papa." And Peter was gone.

When Elise finished eating, she pulled on her rubber boots over her leather button-up ankle boots and took her fitted coat from the front hall tree. A flowing cloak would never do for sled riding. When she was bundled up, Samuel was still talking to Papa. She'd heard Samuel say many times that he would someday be a great politician like Lincoln. "Great politicians have the power to change the world," he would tell her.

Elise, however, didn't feel her older brother was cut out to be a politician. But she held her peace. After all, what did girls know about such things? And that's just what Samuel would tell her if she broached the subject.

On her way out, she stopped in the kitchen to ask Berdeen for a carrot to feed her horse.

"I declare, Elise, you be spoiling that horse of yours more with each passing day."

"He's worth a lot more than a carrot or two," Elise replied. She loved her horse with a passion. When the war started and Papa learned of the desperate need for good breeding stock, he sold off much of his fine herd in order to help the cause. Elise had been only seven at the time. She recalled crying herself to sleep, thinking Papa might sell her horse while she slept. She told the agonizing fear to no one.

Of course Papa never sold Dusty Smoke, but it made her more protective of the horse. Although Chancy did a fine job, she still checked on Dusty every day. Sometimes twice a day. With the carrot Berdeen gave her and an apple to boot, she headed out the back door.

The brilliant sunshine on the white snow was almost blinding as she walked across the porch and down the steps into the deep snow. Immediately, there was the feeling of cold on her ankles in spite of her long wool stockings. She carefully tried to step in the tracks that Peter had made. It made the going somewhat easier.

The stable was cozy warm with the wonderful sounds and smells of horses—one of Elise's favorite places in the whole world.

"Morning, Chancy."

The shy boy mumbled a reply but didn't stop his work of

mucking out the stalls. Peter was sitting on the floor, waxing the runners of their big sled with a piece of beeswax.

"We're gonna fly down that hill," he said as Elise approached. The excitement fairly bubbled in his voice. "Do you think Samuel will take me down once?"

"I'm sure he will," Elise assured him. She hurried past him to go to Dusty's stall. "Dusty," she called out. "Good morning, Dusty. I've brought you something."

Dusty swung her head about at the sound of Elise's voice. The silvery-gray mare wasn't a large horse. Papa's love for the Arabians showed in all the Brannon line. The breed was distinguished by the long, finely arched neck and high-set tail, which went like a flag at the least move—and Dusty had the best of those attributes.

Elise reached out and offered Dusty the carrot, feeling her horse's soft breath caress her hand. The carrot was gone in a moment, and Dusty lifted her head over the stall, snuffling about for more. Elise laughed. "What makes you think there's more?" she teased.

Just then Samuel was beside her. "You have that horse as pampered as a house pet."

Elise extended the apple on the flat of her hand. "I could only wish she *were* a house pet. Think she'd do well in the playroom?"

Samuel grinned. "Only if it didn't give Berdeen a case of dyspepsia." He stepped over to the next stall, where his horse, Vardan, was stabled. The roan gelding stood taller than Dusty and was more boisterous. Mama always said his heart was full of run.

"Come on, you two," Peter called anxiously. "Let's get to the hill before the whole neighborhood arrives."

"He's right," Samuel said. He reached out to grab Elise's arm and pulled her along. "Come on, sis. Let's go!"

Elise could only giggle as she ran to keep up. "Bye, Dusty," she called out. "I'll be back after a while!"

They put Peter on the sled, and Elise and Samuel pulled the sled up the road to where the ridge offered a clear slope with few trees and no houses. It was the favorite sledding area in the neighborhood, and already there were a few sledders shouting as they zoomed down the hill.

The first few times, all three Brannon children loaded on their sled, with the two boys sandwiching Elise between them. She wasn't sure if they wanted to protect her or whether Peter purposely enjoyed falling off the back into the deep powdery snow. Samuel held the rope and worked the steering mechanisms. She held on to Samuel's sides, clutching handfuls of his thick coat, and buried her face into his back. They sailed down so fast that it sucked her breath out of her lungs. She tried not to squeal, but she couldn't help it.

They laughed and giggled as they pulled the sled back up the hill. Peter begged to go alone, but Samuel kept saying he'd better not. "You're not old enough to handle such a big sled all by yourself," Samuel said.

As a consolation, Samuel set Peter in front of him, and the two went down with Peter steering. But that only made him more determined to go alone. "I can do it," he insisted. "I bet you were going down alone when you were eight. You didn't have any older brother to help."

"No, I didn't," Samuel agreed, "but Cousin Alan kept a close watch over me."

But in the end, Peter's begging won over Samuel's soft heart. Samuel looked at Elise and raised his brows. Elise shrugged in response. She figured Samuel had gone down the hill alone when

25

he was much younger than eight, but she kept quiet, feeling it should be his decision.

"Oh, all right. One time," Samuel said. "But be very careful, and remember to steer clear of those trees at the bottom."

But Peter wasn't listening. "Hurrah," he shouted. "I'll fly faster all by myself!" He turned the sled to aim it down the hill just right. Then he settled himself on it, bracing his feet on the steering bars. "Give me a push, Samuel. A big old push."

Samuel did as Peter asked, giving a shove that sent his younger brother careening down the hillside. Peter was doing fine, squealing with delight as he went. Suddenly, from out of nowhere, another sled carrying three bigger boys came flying down beside him. Elise's breath caught as she saw them. They should have waited.

"Look out, Peter!" Samuel called out. But it was too late. The presence of the other sled frightened and confused Peter, causing him to veer sharply away. With a great crash, he hit a small tree and tumbled into the snow.

Elise and Samuel went running down the hill, calling their brother's name as they ran.

CHAPTER 3

Letters to Soldiers

Samuel reached him first. "Peter, are you all right?"

Peter tried to sit up and gave a groan. "It's my ankle."

"Don't move," Samuel instructed. "Lie still so I can look."

Elise saw Peter's face wince with pain. "Those big kids should know better," she scolded.

"They have as much right to the hill as we do," Samuel told her. "Peter, old boy, you should have kept going straight. They weren't going to hit you."

"It scared me when I saw them," he said. "Ouch!" He reached down to hold his ankle. "It hurts bad."

Elise helped Samuel to set the sled aright, then they carefully lifted Peter up on it. Samuel pulled up Peter's trouser leg and eased down the woolen stocking. "It's swelling already," he said. Samuel sat down in the snow and pulled off his own shoe and stocking. Then he filled his stocking with snow. He packed the icy woolen stocking about Peter's ankle.

Peter grimaced, but he didn't complain.

"There," Samuel said, pulling his shoe back on over his bare foot. "That'll help to keep the swelling down till we get you home."

"We can't pull him up the hill," Elise said.

Just then the older boys came running back up the hill. "I told Jay not to take it down at that moment," one of them said.

"We're sorry," said another. "Is he hurt bad?"

"His ankle," Samuel answered.

"We'll help you get him back up," said the one named Jay. Each of the four older boys took a corner of the long sled and lifted it like a stretcher. That put a smile on Peter's face, in spite of his pain. Elise followed behind, pulling the other boys' empty sled.

The boys were impressed that Samuel knew to make a cold pack out of his sock, but it didn't surprise Elise. She'd seen him work with horses in the same gentle manner that he was using with Peter. It seemed to be second nature to him. Other horse owners—friends of Papa's—often called on Samuel when their horses were ailing or hurt. They nicknamed him *the young horse doctor*.

The boys offered to help Samuel and Elise take Peter home, but Samuel said they could easily pull him on the roadway. He thanked the boys as though it hadn't been their fault at all. "It was nice of them to come back and help," he said as they pulled the sled homeward.

Elise just wished they'd been more careful in the first place, but she said nothing. Peter insisted over and over that he would have done fine if the big boys hadn't come by. Samuel kindly agreed with him.

Peter's sprain turned an ugly purple, but his older brother's quick thinking prevented much swelling. By the time Verly came over that afternoon, Peter was hobbling about with the aid of a crutch that Mama had retrieved from the attic.

He played soldiers in the corner of the playroom while Verly and Elise set up the table for tea.

"You're a good sport to go sledding with your brothers," Verly said to Elise as they arranged the dolls on the extra chairs.

"It's great fun," Elise replied. "It fairly takes your breath away."

"Doesn't it frighten you—speeding so fast?"

Elise set out the doll cups and saucers on the table. "Not frightening exactly. More like a delicious excitement." But she could see her quiet friend wasn't too convinced.

"Alexander, being nine years older than me, treated me more like a little doll than a sister." Verly picked up the china doll and smoothed its silken dress. "We didn't play much together."

"Elise and I play together a lot," Peter said from his side of the room, "and now I can beat her in checkers all the time."

Elise smiled. "He does, too."

"It must be fun to have someone to play with." Verly glanced about the room. "And in such a nice playroom."

Elise felt badly that Verly, and her mother had been forced to sell their home. The room they rented at Aunt Ella's was smaller than the Brannon playroom.

"But you have us," Peter put in.

Elise was pleased at Peter's thoughtfulness, but she knew it wasn't the same. To Verly, she added, "We do want you to come whenever you can. It's fun to have another girl around. Peter doesn't much like to play dolls."

The door opened then, and Berdeen came in with the tea cart. "Teatime it is, for a bonny lad and two bonny lassies," she said in her lilting brogue. "Shall we set up on the doll table?"

"Oh yes, let's," Verly answered. "That is, if it's all right."

"Of course it's all right," Elise assured her.

Peter had shot down all his soldiers and was setting them up again in neat rows. "I'm having mine right here on the floor. The general can't leave his troops."

"If it warn't for ye hurt fut, I'd never let you get away with such a thing," Berdeen said.

"It's not my foot, it's my ankle," Peter corrected her. "I'm pretending I got hurt in the war."

"Peter," Elise scolded, "that's a terrible thing to play." Turning to Verly, she said, "How I wish the war were over and done with."

"Dearie me, I do, as well," Berdeen said, transferring the tray from the cart to the small table. "Sure and it's been a dreadful long and drawn-out affair."

"If there'd been no war, I'd still be living in our own house with my own room and back at my old school," Verly said softly. "And Papa would still be alive."

"Do forgive me, wee lassie," Berdeen said, all flustered. "I dinna intend to make you think of sad things."

"Please, don't apologize," Verly insisted. "I think of it all the time anyway."

"I would, too, if I were you," Elise agreed gently. "I know I would."

"Where is your dear brother, lassie?" Berdeen asked.

"The letter we received just before Christmas was from Chattanooga, Tennessee, where he serves with General Rosecrans. It was written back in September."

Berdeen's face grew pale. They'd all heard of the terrible fighting in and around Chattanooga all during the autumn.

"I have an idea," Elise said, wanting to break the spell of gloom that had come into the room. "After teatime, let's write letters. You write to Alexander, and I'll write to Uncle George."

Verly's face brightened. "That's a fine plan."

"I'll run down and ask Mama for stationery and envelopes," Elise offered.

"No need for you to bother when I'll be tripping down myself," Berdeen said. "I'll fetch the writing things to you when I come back for the tea cart."

"Thank you, Berdeen," Elise said.

The girls had a grand time pretending they were grown ladies, serving tea and cakes to one another and the dolls. Peter, of course, pretended he was doling out army rations to his soldiers. Looking up from his games, Peter said, "In Uncle George's letters, he says the army food is awful."

"Alexander tells us the same thing," Verly agreed as she sipped tea from a dainty cup.

"That's why Mama helps Aunt Ella and Cousin Melissa at the Soldiers' Aid Society," Elise said. "They pack crates of good things to eat and send them by train to the battlegrounds. Mama told us they sometimes pack jars of fruit and jams in corn-meal. The cornmeal keeps the jars from breaking, and then the soldiers can cook gruel or pone with the cornmeal. Isn't that a clever idea?"

"My mama would help at the society, too, but she has to work to pay our rent." Verly's voice was sad again. "Some nights she sits up sewing long after I'm asleep. I wish she didn't have to work so hard."

"I wish so, too," Elise agreed. "Have another cake?"

Taking the little cake, Verly said, "I'm going to study very hard, and when I'm old enough, I'll hire out as a schoolteacher and help Mama with the money I earn."

Elise had never thought about having to earn money. What a terrible thing to have to be concerned with when Verly wasn't even eleven.

Just then, Berdeen returned to take the tea tray. In her hand were the sheets of stationery and envelopes. Once the tea things were cleared away, the girls spread their work out on the table.

The room was quiet except for the scratching of their pens as they wrote letters to the men who were so far away fighting a terrible war. Elise glanced over at Peter. He'd fallen asleep on the floor with his head resting on his arm. She smiled and went back to her letter.

After a few moments, Verly looked over at Elise's letter. "Whatever are you doing?" she said. "You're messing up your pretty letter with those silly drawings."

"I like to draw silly things in my letters to Uncle George. I do the same thing for my cousin Jeremiah."

"Why?"

Elise looked at her friend. "Because I think they need something to laugh about."

"But war is a serious thing. The men are doing a great service for their country."

"All the more reason for them to laugh. I don't just draw silly pictures. I put in a few riddles, as well."

"You put riddles in your letters?" The serious Verly was incredulous.

"Sure. I ask the riddle, and when Uncle George writes back, he lets me know if he can figure out the answer. Sometimes he asks the other soldiers if they know the answers."

"Tell me one of the riddles," Verly said, her chin in her hand.

"All right. Can you tell me what belongs to yourself and yet is used by everybody else more than yourself?"

"Something that belongs to me but everybody else uses? I haven't any idea. What is it?"

Elise giggled. "It's your name."

Verly gave a little chuckle. "That's good. Of course. My name. I like your riddle."

Elise told a couple more riddles, which also made Verly laugh. "See what I mean?" Elise said. "They make you want to laugh. And the Bible says that "a merry heart doeth good like a medicine." Don't you think Alexander would like some of that good medicine?"

"Do you mind if I borrow one of your riddles in my letter?"

"Not at all," Elise told her. As she watched Verly add the riddle to the letter, Elise thought that perhaps Verly needed cheering almost as much as her older brother who was out on the battlefield.

CHAPTER 4

The Traitor!

The streets of downtown Cincinnati were floating in dirty slush. Elise hated that the lovely, pristine snow turned into such a dreadfully sloppy mess. She could feel water soaking the hem of her long skirts as she hurried to keep up with Berdeen. Even Peter on his bad ankle could move through the slush faster than Elise in her hoop skirts.

In the month since Peter's accident, his ankle had healed slowly. When school resumed after the holidays, he was still on a crutch, which made the other boys want to play with the crutch, as well. Now at the close of February, he still had a bit of a limp.

Berdeen was doing the Saturday marketing and needed their help to carry purchases as she bustled about from store to store. Her exasperation knew no end as she discovered one item after another was unavailable because of the war.

"No coffee, no sugar, precious little tea," she muttered to herself as they plunged through another puddle to cross busy Fourth Street. "I can find nary a bolt of good-quality cotton fabric in the entire city. A disgrace, that's what it is. An everlasting disgrace."

Peter looked over at Elise and grinned. Berdeen went through this speech every time they went marketing. Elise couldn't help but feel sorry for Berdeen. She tried her best to keep house and cook for an active family of five, and it wasn't easy with so many shortages.

Only that morning Mama had said, "What I wouldn't give for a good cup of strong coffee." But there was none to be had.

Elise's warm woolen cloak was wrapped snugly about her, and her hood covered her head, but still she felt the icy wind piercing the cloth. She'd be quite relieved to get home and get out of her wet things. Her arms ached from carrying the purchases. Then she remembered what she'd heard about ladies in the South, some of whom were selling their lovely, expensive frocks to buy food. Here in Cincinnati, they still had money and still had their clothes. She knew she should be grateful.

"This here'll be our last place," Berdeen announced over her shoulder. She turned into Walker's Grocery at the far end of Fourth Street. After the shopping was finished, they would go to Papa's office, and Samuel would drive them home in the carriage.

The aromas of pickled herring, soda crackers, apples, and pickles met her as Elise walked past the open barrels in front of the counter. Mr. Walker turned from where he was stocking shelves to hail them with a hearty greeting. "Good day to you, Miss O'Banion. And to you, too, Elise and Peter. Looks like the snow is finally beginning to melt. Won't be long till spring now."

"Not long a'tall," Berdeen agreed. "If'n a body doesn't drown in the street first, I'll be glad to see the springtime come."

Elise and Peter gave polite greetings, as well. Then Berdeen walked back to the butcher counter and ordered a slab of bacon to be sliced. The friendly butcher, Mr. Stefano, laughed and joked with Berdeen as he pulled the slab from the case and threw it on the chopping board to make slices with his large knife.

Elise, not too terribly interested in bacon, joined Peter at the candy counter. As she did, she noticed a man walk into the grocer's. There was something about his expression that held Elise's attention and touched her heart deeply. Sadness etched his face. In this awful time of war, many people had faced terrible losses. It must be so with this man.

Elise waited to hear Mr. Walker sing out his greeting. Instead, he glanced at the man and returned to stocking the shelves. She could hardly believe her eyes. Why would he do such a thing? The man was not old, but his wide shoulders beneath a worn cloak drooped with a weight too heavy to bear. He came a bit farther into the store, as though testing ice on the river. Except for Berdeen's chattering in the back, all was quiet. Peter gazed at the candy, picking out his choices. Tin cans clinked as Mr. Walker fastened his attention on the shelves and kept his back to the customer.

The man had removed his hat, and his eyes scanned the store. Before Elise could think to look away, their eyes met and locked. His hazel eyes were not angry or bitter; rather they were filled with profound sadness. He seemed to give a deep sigh. Then he replaced his hat and walked slowly out the door.

It had all happened in a matter of a few moments, but it seemed like an eternity. She turned back to the candy case.

"The selection is getting smaller all the time," Peter muttered, not unlike Berdeen. "Before this old war is over, there might not be any candy at all."

The packages of bacon and salt pork were wrapped in brown butcher paper. Berdeen placed them on the front counter, and Mr. Walker wrote up the ticket and put it with the Brannon account.

"Thank you kindly for your business, Miss O'Banion," he said.

"What about the candy, Berdeen?" Peter insisted. "We get candy, don't we?"

Berdeen gave a little snort. "Candy you be a-wantin'. Rotted teeth is what you'll be a-gettin'."

"But Mama said—"

"The missus spoils you terrible bad, but there's nary a thing I can do about it." She gave a wave of her hand. "Pick what poison you'll have today."

Peter grinned at Elise. Berdeen always went on about not wanting to be responsible for their teeth falling out. But Elise knew they didn't eat that much candy. To begin with, Mama wouldn't allow it. Secondly, there just wasn't that much extra money for luxuries these days.

When they were out on the sidewalk once again, Elise asked, "Who was that man who came in to shop, Berdeen?"

"What man?"

"Didn't you see him? He came inside and waited a moment, but Mr. Walker wouldn't speak to him, so he left."

"Ah, you've heard of him, lassie. That would be Mr. Milton Finney. His son went off fighting for the South, and nary a soul in the city will have a thing to do with him."

"But that's not right. *He* didn't join the Rebels."

"I know how you must see it, darlin', but feelings are hot and not given to reason in wartime. People look at him and wonder if his son has shot one of their sons. It's wretched, but that's how it is."

Elise slowed her pace as she thought about such a horrible thing. Then she had to hurry through the puddles to catch up again. "Where does he live?" Elise wanted to know.

"Are you meanin' to tell me you never laid eyes on the man riding by your own house?"

Elise shook her head. Both her bedroom and the playroom were situated at the back of the house. She certainly didn't see all the traffic that went by.

"I never did. He lives by us? In Walnut Hills?"

"Farther into the woods, in a small cabin. Moved up there a few months ago."

"By himself?"

"Naturally, by himself. Now pray tell who would want to live with a traitor?"

"But he's not a traitor—his son is."

"Dinna matter. I tell ye again, lassie, there's no reason in wartime."

"I think I've seen him." Peter spoke up. "Does he ride a speckled gray horse, and he rides sort of bent over in the saddle?"

"That's him," Berdeen said. "See there? Your brother's seen the man."

"But I didn't know he was a traitor."

"Peter!" Elise said. "He's *not* a traitor."

"But Berdeen just said—"

"She was just saying what people *think* of the man, not what he truly is."

"Aye, laddie. Elise is right. None of us may ever know what or who he truly is."

The sign on Papa's office door read BRANNON LAW FIRM. Samuel had often said to Elise that he dreamed of the day when that sign would be changed to BRANNON & BRANNON LAW FIRM when he entered the profession, too. Papa's friend Salmon Chase had often told Papa how relieved he would be when the war was over and his duties in serving on Lincoln's cabinet in Washington, D.C., were finished so he could come home again.

Samuel was out running an errand, so they had to wait a few minutes, but none of them minded. They warmed their feet by the stove in the reception area and relished a few moments of rest. Papa was in with a client, so he wasn't even able to say a proper hello to them. Frank, Papa's clerk, offered them cups of tangy hot cider, which helped to warm their insides.

Presently, Samuel came breezing in the door. "Hello, all," he said, touching his hat. Under his arm were packets of documents, which he laid on Frank's desk. He'd been to the courthouse delivering and fetching needed papers for Papa's work.

"Peter, come help me get Aveline hitched to the carriage, and I'll get you home." He surveyed the three of them for a moment. "You look a little peaked."

"It's cold, the streets are full of slush, I can't find proper supplies, and we're footsore," Berdeen said. "I wager that'd serve to make a body appear a bit peaked all right."

Samuel smiled. "Your coach'll be ready in a jiffy."

"I'd be most obliged," she answered.

On the way home, Elise couldn't stop thinking about Milton Finney. If no one would wait on him, how could he ever purchase food? How could he live so closed off from the rest of the world? *It must be terribly lonely,* Elise thought.

Peter fumbled about in Berdeen's shopping bag and pulled out the bag of candy. Then he offered everyone a piece. Elise sucked on a peppermint stick and wondered where Mr. Finney's cabin was located. Perhaps Samuel knew. But then she thought better of asking him. Or anyone else for that matter. Berdeen was right about there being no reason in this long war. People were full of hate and suspicion. She'd just take a ride after the spring thaw. Walnut Hills wasn't that big. She'd find the cabin on her own.

At the Brannon house, Samuel pulled the carriage close to the back kitchen entrance so they could all help Berdeen with the parcels and baskets. As they were putting things away, Mama came into the kitchen.

"Ah, how good it is to see my children being such kind helpers to Berdeen."

"Aye, ma'am. They're hearty troopers, the lot of them."

Mama's hands were behind her back. "I have a little surprise for such good workers," she said.

Peter ran to her. "A surprise for all of us?" He tugged at her arm. "What is it?"

"Guess which hand," she said. Peter tapped one, but she shook her head. Then he tapped the other, and she pulled out a handful of tickets. "We're going to the National Theater this evening."

"Hurrah!" Peter cried out. "A night at the theater!"

Samuel wasn't quite as excited, but Elise was thrilled. How she loved the large, old theater that was the pride of Cincinnati. Papa, who'd seen the famous Drury in London, said the National far surpassed the Drury. Some old-timers fondly called Cincinnati's theater "Old Drury."

Looking at Elise, Mama added, "I've a bit more to add to the surprise. There are two extra tickets. Do you think Mrs. Boyd and Verly would want to accompany us?"

Elise felt like squealing. "Oh, Mama, they never get to go anywhere special. Not like the theater. It'll be such a treat for them both. Thank you for thinking of them."

"I'll be going back to town now," Samuel said. "Should I stop by to let them know?"

"Yes, Samuel," Mama said, "please do. Tell them we'll fetch them at half past eight."

Elise could hardly believe this delightful news. What a bright spot this would be for Verly and her mama. How she wished she could relay the message herself.

Since Elise knew Verly would be self-conscious about her lack of fancy dresses, Elise opted not to wear her best pink silk. Instead she chose a church dress of navy poplin with white lace trim. Still a nice dress, it was not nearly as fancy as the silk.

When she came down the stairs, Mama looked at her, studied the dress a moment, then smiled. She understood. Elise released a little sigh of relief.

If Verly was worried about her clothes, it was a short-lived worry. The two girls sat together in Papa's large carriage, laughing and talking as they drove from Walnut Hills into the city. When they stopped in front of the grand building on Sycamore Street, Verly's eyes grew wide. "I've been by here many times, but I've never been inside."

"You've never been to a play?" Elise asked.

Verly shook her head. "Only little skits and dramas at school."

Papa and Samuel assisted each of them as they stepped down from the carriage and went up the stairs and into the vast lobby. Verly gazed about at the marble floors, the gold-leaf ceilings, and heavy glistening chandeliers full of glowing candles.

"Papa was never interested in such things as the theater," Verly whispered to Elise. Then she paused. "But I'm not criticizing him," she added quickly.

"Of course not," Elise assured her. "Different people like different things. I'm so glad Mama and Papa love the theater, because I do, too!"

After Papa had taken care of the team and the carriage, he joined them, and they all went upstairs to their special balcony seats. Verly touched the velvet seats and smiled at Elise. "I'm so pleased you invited us."

"It was Mama. She's the one who thought of it."

The drama was powerful and moving. Elise considered it to be a perfect remedy for forgetting about the war for a few short hours. During intermission, as they stood about in the crowded lavish lobby, Elise said to Verly, "Isn't it amazing how the lively drama on the stage can help people forget their troubles?"

Verly nodded. "You're right. This is the happiest night I've had in a long, long time. It's certainly helped me to forget about my troubles."

Elise thought about that for a moment. "Verly, let's you and I write a play together. Perhaps we could use it to cheer sad people."

Verly's face brightened. "Write a play? Together? Why, that's a splendid plan."

"Come, girls," Mama said, shooing them back in. "The second act is about to begin."

"We can begin it next week," Elise whispered as the lights went low and the curtain rose.

CHAPTER 5

Cabin in the Woods

Mrs. Boyd couldn't stop thanking the Brannons for their thoughtfulness in including her and Verly in the festive evening. As Papa and Samuel escorted the Boyds from the carriage to the front steps of the Harvey Boardinghouse, Elise felt all warm and happy inside. Bringing joy to other people, she decided, was about the best feeling in the world.

She and Verly now had a secret because they'd promised each other that they wouldn't tell a soul about their play until they were ready to begin casting. The next morning at church, they made funny faces at one another across the aisle. Verly and her mama always sat in the Harvey pew. Aunt Ella, Melissa, and the twins treated them more like family than boarders.

Elise was sure that must ease Mrs. Boyd's burden somewhat. But life was still difficult for the widow. Elise hoped they would soon receive a letter from Alexander so their hearts would rest easy once again. Elise couldn't imagine how awful it would be to have Samuel gone and not know where he was or even if he was alive.

This Sunday, Aunt Ella's elder son, Charles, sat with the family. Charles's work with the Little Miami Railroad kept him away from the city a good deal of the time. Trains were constantly moving supplies and troops and bringing the wounded home. Elise knew Charles's life was in danger in his locomotive just as much as the soldiers fighting out on the battlefields. He told many stories of being shot at and having railroad bridges blown up.

His bride-to-be, Alison Horstman, sat primly by his side. Their wedding was set for spring—that is, if Charles could get a day or so of leave. Alison's father, Ted Horstman, was an executive for the Little Miami, and it was he who introduced the tall, handsome, quick-thinking Charles to his youngest daughter.

Elise looked at Alison, who was as pretty as her name. How fortunate she was to be getting a husband during these times. Elise had heard Cousin Alicia say that by the time she was ready to be married, all the young men would have been killed in battle.

After services, the cold gray of the day prevented churchgoers from doing much visiting in the churchyard. Everyone wanted to get home and get warm. But Elise and Verly captured a few minutes to talk.

"I've been so full of ideas for a play," Verly said, "that I could barely sleep last night."

"That's good. We'll need lots of ideas."

"Have you ever written a play before?"

Elise shook her head. "Never. But I've read plenty of them. It can't be too hard. And we'll want to create enough parts so several of our friends can help us put it on."

"Let's begin tomorrow at recess." Verly looked up at the sky. "Looks like it'll be an indoor day."

"And remember, we want to keep it a secret."

Verly smiled. "That'll be the most fun part."

During recess for the next couple weeks, Elise sat with Verly as they penned scene after scene. Their story was about an Ohio backwoods farmer, his wife, and several children and their funny escapades on the farm.

"They'll talk funny," Elise said, "like the Squirrel Hunters who came to Cincinnati during the siege." Though she'd been only eight at the time, she remembered helping to serve food to the hundreds of backwoodsmen who rushed to defend the city when Rebels threatened attack.

"A good idea," Verly agreed. "They'll say things like, 'I was sartain them peaches was spiled.' "

Elise laughed. "You're good at that. Do some more."

"How about this: 'The dogs follered the coons right close, but we brung no meat home cuz the crick was up.' "

Elise put her hand over her mouth to stifle the giggles. "Do you think you can teach that to our actors?"

Verly thought a minute, then shrugged. "I don't see why not. It's pretty easy once you get the hang of it."

"I heard the Squirrel Hunters, too, but I never picked up on the way they talked like you did."

Verly smiled shyly at the praise.

When Verly first came to Walnut Hills Elementary School, she'd kept mostly to herself. The loss of her home and her father had broken her heart. Now here she was laughing and becoming excited about their play. Elise's plan to cheer up sad people through her play was working even before the play was presented. Miss Earles seemed pleased as well to see Verly so interested in something.

Whenever Miss Earles took her long rod and pulled down the map of the United States, Verly's face would go white. She'd told Elise one day that her papa was buried near a town in Virginia. Her mama grieved that they couldn't even visit Papa's grave.

The map of the war was changing. The Union now held the

entire Mississippi River, cutting off the Confederate states from Texas and from their supply bases on the river. Even though many of the students had lost brothers, cousins, fathers, and uncles in the war, Miss Earles felt it should be discussed and that they be kept informed of what was happening.

On a separate map on the far wall, she had the children write on tiny slips of paper the names of their soldier-relatives. These were then pinned to the map in the place where that person was fighting. The map was getting quite full of strips of paper. Each morning after Miss Earles read from the Bible, they prayed for the names on their map.

"You are living in a time of history that is changing our entire nation," Miss Earles told them one day. "It's vital that you learn from it as much as you can."

Elise wasn't so sure she agreed. Though she wanted to pray for Uncle George and Cousin Jeremiah, she wished she could ignore the terrible war altogether!

Spring was ushered in by downpours of cold rain. Every day, Elise thought about Mr. Finney, the man she'd seen in the grocer's in February. She wanted so much to go find his cabin, but she knew Mama wouldn't let her go riding alone when the weather was so nasty.

Most afternoons after school, Elise and Peter helped Chancy walk the horses. One of the mares—Mama's favorite, Allegro— was getting ready to foal, and they were all excited about the new arrival. Mama always said there was nothing like the sight of a foal in the paddock to make the heart glad.

In another week or so, Chancy would turn the horses outside

every day, but Papa never liked his best horses to be out until the weather was warmer.

One afternoon when Elise and Peter arrived home from school, the sun was shining and there was a tinge of warmth in the air. This was the day she planned to locate Mr. Finney's cabin, but she knew it wouldn't be easy to slip away from Peter.

After changing from their school clothes and grabbing apples for the horses, they raced one another out to the stable. In her apron pocket, Elise carried a note for the man accused of being a traitor, but she wasn't sure what she was going to do with it.

Chancy was walking Allegro in the paddock. His plaid blanket coat was slung over one of the fence posts, and his long-sleeved red woolen underwear showed beneath his worn shirt. The too-large trousers, looking like hand-me-downs, were held up by plain gray suspenders. Chancy was gentle with Allegro, and it made Elise thankful that he was caring for their horses.

Elise climbed up on the paddock fence to watch for a moment. In her hand, she held her broad-brimmed straw hat by its ribbons. Berdeen had reminded her to be sure to wear her hat, but the warm sunshine felt delicious on her head, and Elise didn't want to block that warmth with her hat.

"When do you think she'll foal?" Elise called out to Chancy.

"Looks to be soon, Miss Elise. This week maybe."

"I can't wait," Peter said, climbing up beside her. "I'm old enough now—I can help train it."

"That would please Papa," Elise told him, turning to go inside. She went to Dusty's stall and fed her the apple, which the horse ate greedily. "You look like you're ready to stretch your legs," Elise whispered into the long, twitching ear. After giving the horse a good brushing, she took her into a paddock and walked her for a while.

Peter did the same with his horse, Aleron.

As casually as she could, Elise said, "I believe I'll saddle up and take a short ride."

"Good idea," Peter said. And as Elise expected, he added, "I'll do the same and join you."

"Aleron will appreciate the exercise, I'm sure," she said, "but Peter, would you please ride somewhere other than where I do?"

The disappointed look on her little brother's face made Elise wince. "Why?" he asked.

"I need to be alone," she explained lamely. "I have some things that need pondering."

"Does your pondering have to do with all those papers you and Verly have been writing? You've sure been secretive about it."

Elise thought a moment. "In a way it does, yes." She led Dusty toward the back stable doors. "And Peter, I want you to know our secret writing is going to include you."

Peter's face brightened. "You don't say. Truly?"

"It'll be a few weeks yet, but you'll be included."

That seemed to appease him, and he continued walking Aleron around the paddock. Elise hurried inside, saddled Dusty Smoke, tied on her hat, and mounted up. She hadn't lied to Peter because some way, somehow, she fully intended to invite poor Mr. Finney to come to see their play.

As she rode down the lane to the road, she realized she wasn't sure how she would find Mr. Finney's cabin. But even if she never found it, she was happy to be out riding and enjoying the first signs of spring. The area past their house was largely undeveloped and featured thick stands of trees, each of which was beginning to sport tiny green buds. The road followed the trails that had been here since the first fur trappers came down the Ohio River.

A lively cottontail bunny hopped out in front of Dusty, causing her to stop suddenly and shy sideways, but Elise easily maintained control. She'd been riding for almost as long as she could remember. Even Papa said she was a good horsewoman. "You take after your mama when it comes to horses," he'd said so often.

Before the war, Mama spent almost every waking hour in the stables, working with her favorite mounts. Now she seldom got out to the stables. She was much too weary after working long hours as a volunteer with Soldiers' Aid and at the military hospital. The war had changed everyone and everything.

Elise spied the cabin after she'd been riding for about three-quarters of an hour. It wasn't tucked back into the woods as she thought it might be. It sat only a few feet from the road. The simple planked-over log cabin looked like a relic from the past. There was no smoke coming from the chimney, and there was no gray speckled horse about. She pulled Dusty to a stop and sat for a moment, thinking. From her apron pocket beneath her cloak, she brought out her note. It read:

I don't agree with those who say you're a traitor. I'm sorry they say those things and sorry that you've been treated badly.

A friend,
Elise

Urging Dusty forward, she slowly rode closer to the cabin. A tin washtub hung from a nail on the side wall, and the scrub board hung beside it. A castoff wagon wheel lay beside the rickety front stoop. It appeared that repairs of the stoop were in progress. Fresh-cut lumber lay in a neat stack.

The front dooryard was mostly mud created by the heavy spring rains. Near the back door was a pile of split logs and kindling. The axe was imbedded in a hickory stump where the kindling could easily be split.

"Whoa, Dusty," Elise said softly. All of a sudden, her heart beat wildly. What if the man was here but hiding? What if he was angry and had a gun?

Then she laughed to herself. "Crazy imagination. The man I saw in Walker's wasn't an angry man but a hurt man."

Between the house and the road was a sprawling hickory tree that had a couple rusty nails driven into the trunk. Possibly it had been put there to hang clothesline rope. With the note in her hand, Elise slid off Dusty and hit the ground. Keeping the reins tightly in her hand, she stepped up to the tree. She pressed the note over one of the nails, making a little tear that slipped over the nail head. Stepping back, she looked at it hanging there.

Satisfied, she remounted Dusty and rode home.

CHAPTER 6

A Spring Wedding

A week or so after Elise visited the cabin in the woods, the bells from churches and fire stations began ringing across the city. Silently, she prayed that it was good news. Papa and Samuel came home from town that evening with the news that General Grant had been named general-in-chief of the entire Union army by President Lincoln.

"It's about time," Papa said. He'd long been saying that the president needed to get rid of some of the generals who were only seeking their own glory on the battlefields. Many times Elise had heard Papa say, "We need a military leader who wants the war to be over—period."

This appointment seemed to please Papa very much. A few days later, a letter arrived from Uncle George and echoed Papa's sentiments. After the family finished their evening meal, Mama read the letter to them. Uncle George relayed how pleased the soldiers in and around Memphis were. The letter read:

> *To a man, we are cheering our new leader, General Grant.*
> *The men seem to have been infused with new hope at the*
> *announcement.*
>
> *In February, our troops moved south to meet Sherman in*
> *Meridian in hopes of making a grand destructive swath*

*through the South. But our troops met an angry Nathan
Bedford Forrest, who had brought fresh troops from out west.
That Rebel fights like a maniac. We were told even after
Forrest's own younger brother died in the fighting, it didn't
slow him for a moment.*

*Our men said they saw Forrest have two horses shot from
beneath him, but he grabbed saber and sword and continued to
battle on foot. Men will blindly follow a leader of that sort.*

*We all know that the South cannot hold out much longer.
Their supplies and money are dwindling to a trickle. In spite
of that, you have never seen such bold, daring, fearless fighters.
They are all spunk and grit. It grieves me that their gallantry is
all for naught. There's no way they can win. It's only a matter of
time. And yet so many more lives must be lost in the process.*

"I wish I could go fight," Peter said when the letter was finished.

"Peter," Elise told him, "don't say such things. You'll worry Mama half-sick."

Mama reached over and patted Elise's hand. "He just means he wants to help," she said.

Elise shook her head. "How could anyone *want* to go into those places of killing and dying?"

"Our teacher says it's a cause worth fighting for," Peter replied, puffing his chest out just a bit as he said it.

"Don't you want the slaves to be free, Elise?" This question came from Samuel, who had a serious look on his face.

"Of course I do. And they are now. So why can't the fighting be over?"

Papa said, "If we had that answer, we'd stop the war this minute. The truth is, those Rebels—whom we thought could be put down in a few days—have more fight in them than we ever gave them credit for."

Berdeen came in just then to refill Mama's and Papa's cups of tea and to gather the dirty plates.

"It's me own brother who sed the very same words to me when the bloomin' Rebels first fired on Sumter," she said. "He said 'twould be a long, long war. Ernan was a-knowing more'n all them high-faluting generals put together."

Unlike servants in other homes, Berdeen was free to speak her peace in the Brannon household. Papa never raised an eyebrow at her. She was like part of their family.

"Papa," Samuel spoke up, "may I tell what Secretary Chase said in his letter to you?"

"You may."

"Secretary Chase said too many of the Union officers underestimated the South and therefore didn't start out fighting to win. If they had, the war would have been over by now."

"Hanging onto what might have been," Mama said quietly, "will never change today."

"No," Elise said, "but it sure ought to teach somebody not to let this happen again."

"I doubt it ever will, Elise," Papa said. "I doubt it ever will."

The time Elise and Verly had to spend on play writing lessened as warm, sunny April made its appearance. Mrs. Boyd's orders for sewing increased. She got some piecework contracts from one of the city clothiers that sewed uniforms for the Union soldiers. Even though Aunt Ella let Mrs. Boyd borrow the treadle sewing machine, there was a great deal to do. Verly, of course, had to help. She and

Elise promised each other that they would work on the play only when they were together.

Now that the dogwoods were in bloom and the trees were greening, Elise was on Dusty as much as possible, taking long rides. Every once in a while, she would leave another note on the hickory tree at Mr. Finney's house. She included funny stick drawings and a riddle or two. Since she could not expect him to reply, she penned the answer to the riddle at the bottom of the page.

"What's the difference between a sewing machine and a kiss?" she wrote in her note. Then at the very bottom, she wrote in smaller script: "One sews seams nice, and the other seems so nice." The riddle made her smile. She could only hope it did the same for Mr. Finney and that her thoughts toward him were making his life a little easier.

On occasion when shopping with Berdeen, she would see Mr. Finney about town. She always looked at him and smiled, but he looked away and never acknowledged her. Seeing his sadness made her pray even harder for the war to be over soon.

Saturday, April 23—the day of Charles and Alison's wedding—dawned cloudy. However, by the time the Brannons were in the carriage on the way to the Harvey home, the clouds began to break up and the sun was peeping through.

Verly and Elise had talked about the wedding all week at school. They could hardly wait. It would be such fun to have a festive occasion. Elise was to be among the attendants, and Verly had been asked to serve refreshments.

Verly was at the front door when they arrived. Grabbing Elise's arm, she pulled her aside. "You'll never guess what. Mama has given me this entire day off. She said I've worked so hard, she promises we'll not pick up a piece of sewing until Monday morning."

"What good news! That'll make this day even more special for you." That thought gave Elise an idea. "Say! Why not ask your mama if you can come home with us and spend the night? We'll have time to finish the play!"

Verly's eyes brightened. "Let's ask right now. Mama's upstairs helping with Alison's dress."

Elise followed as Verly led through the crowded parlor to the stairs and up to the room where Alison was getting ready. As she went, Verly said, "I've helped a little bit with Alison's dress. It's lovely, Elise. She told me it belonged to her mother, who died when she was just a little girl. But Alison's mother was so tall that we had to alter the dress a great deal."

"I know she appreciates all your help."

"She does. She's thanked all of us. Your aunt Ella is more like a mother to her than a mother-in-law."

"That sounds like Aunt Ella. Full of love."

The two girls slipped into the crowded room. What a joy it was to see everyone smiling and laughing as they helped Alison adjust her gauzy veil. Verly caught her mother's attention and motioned her to the door.

"Hello, Elise," Mrs. Boyd said. "When did you arrive?"

"We just got here."

"Is the parlor full yet?"

"Full to overflowing," Elise assured her. "What fine work you did on Alison's dress. It fits her perfectly."

"Your aunt Ella did most of the work, and of course Verly helped, as well." Mrs. Boyd put her arm about Verly's shoulder. "Verly's my strong right hand. I don't know what I'd do without her help."

"Mama," Verly said, "since you've given me this day off, may I spend it at Elise's house? And stay the night, as well?" she added.

"Of course you may. That would make a nice time off for you."

The two girls looked at one another and smiled. What fun they'd have on this beautiful spring weekend.

Soon the music started, and it was time to line up and march down the stairway into the parlor. Verly and Mrs. Boyd went down to find a place to sit among the other guests.

As Elise walked carefully down the stairs with a bouquet of fresh-cut flowers in her hand, she felt older somehow as a member of the wedding party. It was an honor to have been asked by Alison and Charles.

After the ceremony and after refreshments had been served to the guests, Alison changed into a tailored blue-worsted traveling dress, and the couple left in Mr. Horstman's carriage.

The railroad executive, who'd become rather wealthy as a result of the war, had presented the couple with train tickets to Columbus, where they would stay the weekend until Charles would have to report back to work.

Elise and Verly stood on the front porch with the other guests waving good-bye to the happy couple. Wistfully, Verly said to Elise, "I wonder if I will ever see Alexander's wedding day."

"Have you received a letter yet?"

Verly shook her head. "Nothing. And it's so frightening. I've heard that many of our soldiers are captured and put in prison camps."

"Verly, you can't let yourself dwell on the worst."

"I know, but I can't help it."

Elise put her arm about her friend. "I wish I could help somehow."

Verly smiled—a weak smile, but a smile nonetheless. "You *have* helped me, Elise. Just by being my good friend."

CHAPTER 7

The Play

Elise and Verly worked on their play all Saturday evening. The play, which they'd titled, "A Pig in a Poke," was filled with funny lines. By Sunday afternoon, the playroom was littered with sheets of paper where they'd copied the pages over and over again.

They discussed whom they would ask to take which parts and when they might schedule the play. Looking at the calendar, Elise suddenly had a great idea. "My birthday!" she said.

"What about your birthday?"

"It's in May. May 21. I'll tell Mama I don't want a party. Instead, we'll invite people to come to our play."

"You'd rather give a play than have a birthday party?"

"I sure would! Come, Verly," Elise said as she headed out of the playroom, "let's tell Mama our plan. It's time for the secret to be told."

Mama was pleased with their plan. They explained how they wanted to present it outdoors on a Saturday evening and ask as many people as possible.

"Samuel can help set up boards on crates to make your benches," Mama suggested.

"And we'll use blankets on the clothesline for our curtains," Verly said.

"You should hear Verly talk like a backwoodsman," Elise told

Mama. "She's going to teach our troupe how to do it. It'll keep everyone laughing." Elise could hardly believe how well her plan was developing.

Chancy came running to the house late one afternoon. "Mrs. Brannon, come quickly. It's time! Allegro is having her foal."

Mama and Elise hurried out to the stable. As they did, the church bells began to toll. As usual, Elise felt knots forming in her midsection. While the bells sounded out news, one never knew if it meant good news or bad. Mama paused for a moment and looked at Elise with concern in her eyes, then hurried on her way to the stable.

Though Mama had worked with many mares during foaling time, she could see right off that Samuel was needed. Even Chancy deferred to Samuel's special ways with a horse in dire need.

"You ride into town," Mama said to Chancy, "and tell Samuel to come home quickly. If Mr. Brannon can't get away from his work, put Samuel on behind you and bring him back."

"Yes'm," Chancy said. And he was gone.

Meanwhile, Mama and Elise continued to work with Allegro, walking her back and forth and talking to her, rubbing her down and keeping her calm.

Elise saw the look of relief in Mama's dark eyes when she heard the carriage driving up the lane. When they saw Samuel and Papa enter the dim stable, Elise knew immediately that something was wrong. Mama did, too.

"What is it?" she asked.

"Another horrible massacre in Virginia," Papa said. "A place called the Wilderness. We can talk about it later."

Samuel was there, and that made all the difference. None of them could have explained what he did differently with horses than any of the rest of them, but no one denied he had a special way with the animals. Papa helped, too, of course. When Allegro finally lay down in her stall, Samuel and Papa got right to work. The foal was coming out all wrong and had to be gently turned. Before midnight, the little colt had slipped out onto the clean hay. Though she was weary, Allegro began licking and cleaning the long-legged chestnut foal. Suddenly, he stood on wobbly legs, falling a couple times before making his way to where he could find nourishment.

Elise marveled at the miracle of a birth and what hope it gave, in spite of the news of all the tragic deaths from the war.

After supper, Papa told of the news from the Wilderness campaign, where more than eighteen thousand men had lost their lives. "They were fighting in a heavily wooded area," Papa explained. He had three different newspapers spread before him where he'd read the different accounts. "The artillery and cannons caused the woods to catch fire. Sounds of the wounded screaming as they burned to death filled the night air," he read.

Mama gasped as he told the details. Peter had tears running down his cheeks. Samuel chewed his lip. Elise could take no more. She couldn't stand the thought of wounded men being burned with no one to help them. She ran from the table out the back door, across the porch, and stopped in the yard, where she promptly lost her supper. Soon Mama was by her side, gathering her in her arms and wiping her face with a cool, damp cloth.

"I'm sorry," Elise whispered.

"Don't be sorry, my darling. It makes all of us sick!"

Later as they prayed together, Peter had the idea to name their new colt Chancellor, after the town of Chancellorsville, which was close to the Wilderness and had also been the site of a brutal battle exactly a year earlier. They all agreed with Peter's choice. Then they grew quiet as Papa prayed.

The next few weeks flew by as the girls chose their actors and actresses and assigned play parts. Verly seemed happier than Elise had ever seen her. Cast members were asked to memorize lines before the first rehearsal. Even Chancy was asked to take a part. In spite of his shyness, he agreed to play the part of an old peddler who plays a trick on the family.

The rehearsals were great fun. Verly patiently taught the backwoods characters to mispronounce all their words. Their attempts at mimicking the Squirrel Hunters' speech prompted plenty of laughter. At times they laughed so hard, they could barely practice the lines.

Elise's twin cousins, Alan and Alicia, played the erstwhile parents, while Peter and the Kilgour sisters played the mischievous children. Samuel would be the parson who drops in at the most inopportune times.

Mama helped not only by serving refreshments at rehearsals, but also by penning the invitations. At one point she asked Elise, "What will be the price of admission? Should they pay something to see the show?"

Elise thought a minute. "Two things. One will be something for use at the military hospital, and the second is a riddle. Everyone must bring a riddle!"

Mama chuckled. "Just as I thought you'd say." And she went back to her work.

Costumes were another fun part. Everyone rummaged through trunks of clothes in their attics to find old castoffs that would do.

The yard was level between the house and the stables and paddocks. From there the land went up into the wooded hills behind the stable and sloped down over a ridge on the far side of the house and yard. The spot made a perfect stage.

Berdeen created a curtain with hooks that clipped over the clothesline so it would slide easily. Elise assigned Berdeen the job of stagehand to open and close the curtain at the right moments.

On the morning of the performance, Elise hardly had time to think of her own birthday. There was too much to do. Mrs. Boyd and Verly walked up from the boardinghouse early in the day to lend a hand. Refreshments would be served afterward, so plenty of help was needed in the kitchen.

As the guests arrived that evening, Mama and Papa took the "tickets." By the time everyone had arrived, there were baskets of items for the convalescing soldiers—everything from combs to stationery. And there were enough riddles to last Elise for a very long time.

Elise kept watch as guests came into the yard and took their seats. She was looking for one certain person. She'd left a note for Mr. Finney, inviting him to come and see the play. The note told where she lived and what time to come. But as she stood before her audience to announce the opening of the first act, he'd not arrived.

Elise sat on the front row with a script in her lap, ready to prompt any actors who forgot their lines. But she wasn't needed. Not only did her troupe remember their lines, but they hammed it up more than they ever had during rehearsals. Laughter rang out through the warm night air and filled the clearing. Even Mr. Horstman—who was usually very solemn—burst out with loud guffaws. The sounds of laughter made Elise happy all the way down to her toes!

As Berdeen closed the curtain after the last act, the people gave a standing ovation. Elise could hardly believe it. Then Papa came to the front and put his arm around Elise and made her stand. Putting his hand up to silence the crowd, he first of all thanked everyone for coming and helping to make Elise's play a success. Then he said, "Many of you don't know that this is Elise's birthday. Rather than have a party, she wanted to present this play for all of you."

Elise felt her face burning as the crowd began clapping. Papa again put his hand up. As he did, Berdeen and Mama came out the back door carrying a cake with candles on it.

"Three cheers for Elise," Samuel called out.

"Hip, hip, hooray!" the crowd yelled. "Hip, hip, hooray! Hip, hip, hooray!" Then they burst into singing, "For she's a jolly good fellow."

Elise blew out her eleven candles, after which Mama and Berdeen set up the refreshment table on the back porch, where guests could file by and load up their plates. And Elise was allowed to be the first one through the line!

As Elise took her plate back to a bench to sit down, Papa's cousin, Ruby Brannon, came over and sat down beside her. Elise had always admired Ruby, who had worked tirelessly at the hospital ever since the war began. Papa and Aunt Ella often told the story of how Ruby had fallen deeply in love as a young girl, but when her betrothed died in California, she threw herself into helping others through nursing. Ruby was short with rather plain features, but somehow she was very beautiful.

"Elise," Ruby said softly, "what a noble and generous thing

you've done here tonight. I can't remember the last time I laughed so much."

"Thank you, Cousin Ruby." Elise couldn't avoid blushing a little at the kind words from this fine lady. "That's what I wanted," she added. "To give everyone a bit of God's medicine—laughter."

Ruby smiled gently. "Would you consider gathering up your troupe and presenting 'A Pig in a Poke' on the hospital grounds for the soldiers? I believe there are many brave men who would gain great benefit from 'God's medicine' as you call it."

At first, Elise wasn't sure what to say. She'd never been to the hospital. Although Mama volunteered there often, Elise could never bring herself to view so much suffering. She truly didn't know how Ruby had done it all these years. "I'm not sure I could do it, Ruby," she said, shaking her head. "I got sick when Papa read a report about the Wilderness Campaign."

"The first thing that happens when you're among them," Ruby assured her, "is that you completely forget yourself. They are all so courageous. But you don't have to answer now. You think about it, talk to the others, and then let me know." Ruby stood to her feet. "I'll go through that refreshment line now before the food's all gone."

Elise studied Ruby's straight back and proud head held high as she strode across the grass. Suddenly, Elise realized how much her cousin had sacrificed, not to mention what the soldiers themselves had given up. How could she have possibly hesitated? She jumped up. "Ruby! Ruby!" she called out, running toward her.

Ruby stopped and whirled around, causing Elise to nearly stumble into her. "I know right now, Ruby. I don't have to think about it. I *do* want to put on the play for the soldiers at the hospital." Elise took a breath. "And I thank you so kindly for the invitation."

"I'll get word to the doctors in charge," Ruby told her, "and let you know a date."

School was out, and the welcome month of June warmed the countryside, bringing carefree summer days. Allegro and Chancellor were free to roam in the pasture just down the hill from the stable. Elise never tired of watching the frisky colt kick up his heels, flick his little whip of a tail, and run about. His antics made her laugh. He was already used to Elise's presence. When she went into the pasture and called Allegro, Chancellor came along right beside her. Elise could already tell he was going to be a good horse.

Now that Peter was nine, he worked at the office with Papa several days a week. While Samuel was given more responsible clerking duties, Peter now swept floors and ran errands. Elise might have been lonely had it not been for the upcoming play presentation. What time she wasn't helping Berdeen about the house, she was revising sections of the play. The thought still plagued her that she might get sick right in the middle of everything! How mortified she'd be if that happened. It took time for Ruby to clear all the red tape with those in official positions at the hospital. Finally they received word from Ruby. They were scheduled for a Sunday afternoon late in June. Now Elise was more nervous than ever.

They rehearsed with much more seriousness now. All the players seemed to sense how important their mission would be. They were more ready to listen to Elise's directions as they went through their lines.

Cousin Alan, along with Papa and Samuel, went to the hospital grounds the day before the performance to rig up a rope for the curtains between two trees. They also arranged plank seats in rows across the grass. Ruby told Elise that some of the men would be too weak to be brought outside.

"We plan to bring out as many as possible. Others will be brought near the windows." Ruby smiled as she added, "Be sure to have your players speak loud enough to be heard up on the third floor."

That made Elise more nervous than ever. Chancy's voice was pretty soft. The night before the presentation, she could hardly sleep. She thought of the note she'd left for Mr. Finney. He hadn't come to the first presentation, but perhaps he would come to this one.

The afternoon of the performance, when the Brannons drove up to the hospital in their carriage, Elise saw nurses and volunteers scurrying about like little ants, bringing beds, cots, and wheelchairs out onto the sloping lawn. Elise felt her stomach tighten in a knot. Mama reached over and patted Elise's arm. "You'll be fine," she said.

And she was. Later she could hardly believe it, but as soon as she stepped down from the carriage and saw her troupe, she quickly went into action. She brought everyone together beneath a shade tree in the far corner of the lot and checked to see if they all knew their entrances and exits.

By the time she was in place to announce the beginning of the play, she hardly noticed the bandages, crutches, canes, and scores of empty sleeves and trouser legs.

As before, she sat in the front row with the script in her lap and marveled at the performers before her. Even Chancy surprised her as he nearly shouted his lines in order to be heard by all.

Then Elise heard the laughter. The delicious sound of laughter reverberated all across the shady lawn. For a moment, it made the pain and grief of war seem far away. Far away, indeed.

CHAPTER 8

Milton Finney

As the summer progressed, all the talk around town was of the upcoming presidential election. At the thought of thousands and thousands of men who'd given their lives, some folks were crying out for peace at any price, which was, as Papa put it, "a ploy to get Lincoln out of office." A ploy that Papa felt would be the downfall of the entire nation.

In mid–June, another massacre occurred at Cold Harbor, Virginia. Thousands of Union soldiers were mowed down within minutes of when the fighting began. It seemed the dying would never end.

That summer, Elise spent many hours riding Dusty Smoke, far from the thoughts, sounds, and news of war. Some afternoons, she filled a canteen with water and rode to the wooded hills outside of town. There she soaked up the peace and quiet and prayed.

She often asked Mama and Papa how God could allow so much pain, suffering, and dying, but no one had any answers for her. When she heard war news, God seemed very far away. But in the quiet, shady woods, He seemed very close.

She didn't ride to Mr. Finney's cabin as much these days. She'd given up hope of ever getting an answer from him. One day while in town, she'd seen people pointing at him and openly calling him a traitor. It was a terrible scene. She didn't blame him for not trusting anyone.

One afternoon a couple weeks after the news of Cold Harbor, Elise was looking through the stacks of riddles she'd received on her birthday. She took up a nib pen and copied two riddles onto a sheet of stationery. The first one read: "What is the best thing to make in a hurry?" The answer was: "Haste."

The next one was one of her favorites: "What is the difference between a politician running for office and a dog going into a kennel?" This being an election year, she felt it very fitting, for the answer was: "One lies to get in; the other gets in to lie."

Below the riddles, she wrote:

I wish you could have seen the production of the play my friend and I wrote. Everyone loved it. I hope these riddles make you smile.

Your friend,
Elise

Putting the paper in her apron pocket, Elise set out to saddle Dusty and ride up to the cabin. It was a perfect summer day with just a little breeze and a few wispy clouds scooting across the blue sky. She tied on her straw bonnet as she rode Dusty down the lane to the road and turned north.

Weeds and grass grew high along both sides of the narrow road. They were coated with layers of gray dust. The orchestra of insect sounds and chorus of bird songs kept her company along the way. Through the trees she heard rustling, and in a clearing she saw a doe with her twin fawns. Elise paused to watch till they bolted and fled. She made several stops in the shade to uncork the canteen and take a drink of cool water; and at the point where a small stream converged with the road, she let Dusty drink, as well.

Elise reined Dusty in at the hickory tree near the cabin and slipped out of the saddle to the ground. As she reached up to the nail to hang her note on it, she heard a noise. Stopping, she stood very still and listened. Perhaps it was an animal. A hurt animal. She pushed the paper onto the nail, then listened again. It was a groan. Looking toward the house, she paused. Should she go closer? Her heart thudded in her chest, making her throat tight and dry.

Dusty's ears twitched and flipped back and forth. "You hear it, too, don't you, girl?" Elise whispered. "What do you think? Should we go have a look?"

The reins still in her hand, she moved cautiously from the hickory tree to the front stoop. Now it came louder. It was a groan. And it came from inside the house.

She tied Dusty's reins and hurried across the bare dooryard and up onto the stoop. "Mr. Finney? Mr. Finney? Are you all right? It's me, Elise Brannon."

There was another low groan. She pressed her ear to the wooden door. She tried the door, but the latch was fastened. Frustrated, she jumped off the stoop and ran to the window. Peering in, she could see Mr. Finney lying on the floor. She couldn't be sure if he was hurt or ill. Pushing at the window, she found it stuck fast. How could he have windows closed in the heat of the summer?

She rapped on the window. Then she saw him raise a hand. Cupping her hands over her eyes, she peered in. He was pointing to the back. The back door. It must be open. She raced around to the back, where the door was standing open. The tall man was lying on the floor with his leg all twisted.

"Oh, Mr. Finney!"

He gave a forced smile through gritted teeth. "Caught under my horse. He fell. Think it's broken."

"You need water?"

He nodded and grimaced again.

Elise looked about the cabin. The water bucket sat on a stand by the cupboards with a dipper in it. Taking the granite dipper, she filled a tin cup and brought it to him. Gently, she tried to help him lift his head to drink. It wasn't easy. She wouldn't make much of a nurse.

"I'll ride into town and get a doctor," she said.

With effort, he took another sip. "Won't do any good," he said with little emotion. "No one will come."

How stupid of her. She'd almost forgotten who this was. "When did it happen?"

"Shortly before you got here. Out back in the woods."

"You came all that way on a broken leg?"

"Didn't have much choice." The tone of his voice and the resolute look in his eye told Elise he'd come to terms with the way things were—that he was powerless to change it.

"My brother can set your leg," she said suddenly. "I'll bring the bucket over here beside you, and then I'll ride to town to fetch him."

At her words, she saw a flicker of light come into Mr. Finney's hazel eyes. It was gone in a flash. "He may not come when you tell him who it is."

"My brother's not like that." She stood and lifted the heavy bucket down from its stand and half-carried, half-dragged it over to him. Then she went to the cot at the far side of the room and pulled off the quilt. It was a pretty quilt. Not at all the kind of quilt she thought he would have.

On the wall by the bed was a large portrait of a beautiful lady. She was standing by an ornate fireplace. The lady was smiling, and there were flowers in her hair, but Elise had no time to look at more. As gently as she could, she lay the quilt over Mr. Finney's bad leg, then brought a pillow for his head. At least she knew to do that much.

Then she went to the cupboard and found a tin of crackers and brought it to him. "I'll be back before you know it," she promised. As she stepped toward the back door, he said softly, "Miss Brannon?"

"Yes, sir?"

"I'm much obliged."

Elise knew better than to run Dusty in the hot weather, but she alternated cantering and walking as she hurried out of Walnut Hills and all the way into town to Papa's office. As she rode, she tried to figure out what she would tell Samuel. Or Papa. How would she get Samuel to come back with her?

When she reached downtown, Papa was in his office with a client. Samuel was sitting at a desk in the outer office, his head bent over the papers. Peter wasn't there—probably out running errands, she figured. Frank and Samuel both looked up at her with surprised expressions as she came in. She'd almost forgotten she had her day dress on. Mama would faint if she ever found out that Elise had come into town dressed so shabbily.

"Elise," Samuel said, jumping to his feet. "What're you doing here?"

"I need you. I mean, we need you. Could you come?"

"It isn't Chancellor, is it?"

"No, no. Chancellor's just fine."

"What then?"

She glanced at Frank. "It's sort of private."

"I'll tell Papa I'm leaving."

"Couldn't Frank do that? We need to hurry."

With that, Samuel laid down his pen and came out from behind his desk. Grabbing his hat, he said to Frank, "Tell Papa I'm needed at home. Be back as soon as I can."

Out at the street, Samuel swung up onto Dusty Smoke, then gave his sister a hand up behind him. As they rode quickly down Third Street, he said, "All right, out with it. What's going on?"

"It's Mr. Finney. He's hurt."

"Where is he?"

"In his cabin."

"Elise Brannon, what were you doing at the cabin of Milton Finney?"

"I was just riding by. But that doesn't matter. His horse fell on him, and his leg is broken. I told him you could set it."

"Did you now? What makes you think I could do a thing like that?"

"I know you can."

Pulling Dusty's reins to turn her about, he said, "We'd do best to fetch a doctor."

"No, Samuel. That'll only waste precious time. He said no one will come, and he must know. You've seen how they treat him around town. He can't help what his son went and did, but he's still suffering terribly."

Pausing for just a moment, Samuel urged Dusty forward. "I hope you know what you're doing."

Elise wasn't all that sure Samuel could set a man's leg. After all, Mr. Finney was a big man. But they had to try. When they got there,

Mr. Finney had passed out from the pain. He lay so still, Elise at first wondered if he were alive.

Samuel knelt down beside the man. Pointing to the water and crackers, he asked, "Did you think of that?"

She nodded.

"And the blanket and pillow?"

She nodded again.

He seemed pleased. From his pocket, he pulled out his knife and slit the leg of the trousers so he could look at the break. As he did, Mr. Finney roused, and his eyes fluttered open.

"Now I understand why women faint," he murmured. "Can't feel much then."

Elise was surprised at his ability to joke at a time like this.

"Got any boards I can use as splints?" Samuel asked.

"Out by the woodshed."

Samuel went out the back door, and Elise could hear him rummaging about.

"Samuel's good with animals," she offered. "He just seems to have a touch about him."

Mr. Finney managed a smile. "Good with animals? That's pretty much in keeping with what folks in these parts think of me."

"You're not an animal!" Elise protested.

Samuel returned with two long, flat boards in his hands. "I'll need you to hold onto something," he told Mr. Finney.

The man nodded. "Help me scoot to the doorway. I can grab hold of the door frame."

Together, Samuel and Elise moved Mr. Finney the short distance to the door, but he couldn't help much. It took all their strength to do it. Then as Mr. Finney held to the door frame, Samuel took hold of the foot of the broken leg and prepared to pull it straight to set it.

"I'll do this as quickly as I can," Samuel told him.

Mr. Finney's face was white. Just the movement to the door had drained him. "Do what needs to be done," he said calmly.

Elise had full confidence in her brother, but even she was surprised at how he yanked the leg with one quick precise movement. Mr. Finney promptly passed out again.

"That's a blessing," Samuel told her. "Find a sheet, Elise, and rip it into strips so I can tie these splints in place."

In the corner at the foot of the bed was a small chest. She opened it to find sheets and blankets stored there. A set of elegant hand-embroidered pillow sacks lay on top. She touched them gently to move them out of the way. She felt guilty rummaging through Mr. Finney's things. The sheets on top were nice, but the ones at the bottom appeared to be more worn. She drew one out and tore the strips as Samuel had instructed her.

The splints were in place and the leg was straight and rigid before Mr. Finney roused again. Looking at the leg, he said, "What a fine doctor you'll make one day."

"I plan to study law."

"Like your father," Mr. Finney said.

"Yes, but I'll take it further than a law office. I'll be in politics."

"Rough game, politics," the man said. To which Elise agreed heartily. She never had thought Samuel would make a good politician.

"Think you can hoist yourself up on a chair now?" Samuel asked Mr. Finney.

"Bring one here, and we'll see."

Elise brought a cane-bottom chair over to Mr. Finney, and she held it steady while Samuel helped him pull himself up on it. It was a chore, but they did it.

"Now," Samuel instructed, "you can use the chair rather like a crutch, and we'll help you over to the cot. You'll need to lie down and rest for a while. The floor's not the best place."

"Didn't have much choice when I first came in," he replied.

His remark made Elise smile.

By the time Elise and Samuel were ready to leave, Mr. Finney was lying comfortably on his cot with food and water nearby.

"I'll bring you some soup tomorrow, Mr. Finney," Elise told him.

"This 'Mr. Finney' thing is about to wear on me, girl. Call me Milt. I'm much more accustomed to that name."

Elise looked at Samuel, and he nodded. "All right, Milt. I'll see you tomorrow."

"Before you go," he asked, "you got any new riddles?"

Elise really liked this man. She thought a moment and then said, "What's the difference between one yard and two yards?"

"I give up. What is the difference between one yard and two yards?"

"A fence."

At that, the pained man chuckled. "That's the best one yet," she heard him say as they went outside and mounted Dusty to ride back home.

CHAPTER 9

Suffering the Consequences

On the way home, Samuel and Elise discussed how they were going to tell their parents about Milt Finney. Samuel seemed to think Mama and Papa would be fair-minded about the matter, but Elise wasn't so sure. Feelings about Southern sympathizers were so strong in the city, and she didn't want her parents to stop her from going to see Milt again. He would need food for the next few days until he could hobble about on his own.

Thankfully, Samuel was right. Papa wasn't home until late, but they explained to Mama what had happened, and she commended them on their compassion.

"What do you think Papa will say?" Elise asked her.

"I'll talk to him first," Mama promised. And she did. Elise was allowed to take food to Milt the next day.

She stayed only a few minutes because he was still very weak. His eyes lit up as she set her basket on the table and began to bring out the goodies that Berdeen had packed inside.

Soup, muffins, fruit, boiled eggs, and even butter and marmalade for the muffins appeared. Watching Elise from his cot, Milt said, "Pretty well worth a busted leg to receive a banquet like this."

Elise wanted to ask how he could be so cheerful when he'd been treated so cruelly, but she refrained. Broaching the subject might be too painful for him. She set a chair near his bed to act as a little table, then put his food there. He was able to prop up on one elbow and do a pretty fair job of polishing off most of it, though he spilled a little of the soup.

"Your ma's a good cook," he said as he finished a muffin in two bites.

"Mama doesn't cook much. Berdeen O'Banion, our housekeeper, does most of it."

"Please pay my kindest respects to Miss O'Banion. And to your parents for allowing you to extend this kind generosity."

"I will. I'll tell them." The imposing portrait on the wall above the cot kept pulling her attention. She couldn't stop looking at the painting—and Milt noticed.

"My wife," he said. "Beautiful, wasn't she?"

"So much more than beautiful. Elegant is closer."

"Yes, so she was, bless her soul. An elegant Southern belle. It's only by God's mercy that she was able to go to be with Him and not have to see our nation ripped apart."

Elise nodded. She rinsed out his soup bowl and straightened things up a bit. Then she put the towels back into the basket. "I must go now, but I'll be back tomorrow."

"Have another riddle for me?"

"Why, of course. What's the nearest thing to a cat looking out a window?"

Milt smiled and thought a moment. "A cat looking out a window? I give up. What?"

"Why, the window, of course." She gave a little giggle, and Milt laughed outright.

"That's a good one. How do you come up with so many riddles?"

"At the play we put on in May, I asked everyone to bring a riddle. That was the price of admission."

"Oh yes. I remember. That was written on my invitation, as well. By the way, thank you very much for inviting me."

"I wish you could have come."

"Oh, but I did. Sort of."

"Sort of?"

"I came through the woods behind your stables. I came as close as I could and heard most of it. I had a very difficult time not laughing out loud, in which case most of your guests would have chased me halfway back up the hill."

Elise knew he was right. "I'm sorry you had to hide, but I'm so pleased you came." She put her basket over her arm and left then. Milt Finney was a very nice man, she concluded on her way home.

Elise never knew for sure how Verly found out about Milt. Eventually, she planned to tell Verly herself. She thought it might take time for Verly to adjust to the idea, but she never expected the reaction that actually came. Verly was nothing short of furious.

Elise had ridden over to the boardinghouse one hot summer afternoon to see if Verly could play. The minute Elise rode up, she knew something was different. Verly was sitting out on the covered porch with a lapful of sewing, but the usually bright greeting Elise had come to expect from her friend was missing.

Though Verly glanced up and saw Elise approaching, she acted as though she hadn't. Elise dismounted, tied Dusty to the hitching post, and walked slowly up the stairs. "Good afternoon, Verly. Can you play?"

"Even if I could, I wouldn't play with you."

"Is something wrong?"

Verly looked up, and the hate in her eyes matched what Mr.

Finney saw every time he rode into town. "You should know if something is wrong," she snapped. "You traitor!"

"I'm not a traitor, Verly. You have no right—"

"I have every right in the world. The son of the man you're helping may be shooting my brother right as we speak."

"Verly, that's crazy talk. Milton Finney has no control over his grown son. Many people left Cincinnati to fight for the South, and many Southerners came to live in Cincinnati after the war started to side with the North."

"For all you know," Verly continued as though Elise hadn't said a word, "that man may be secreting information to his son and spying on important troop movements."

"There haven't been any important troop movements in our city since the siege in '62. All the troops are out on the battlefields."

"That doesn't matter," Verly retorted. "There are still things he could spy about."

"Verly, I came to see if you can play for a while. I didn't come to argue."

"Perhaps if you had a father who was killed by a stinking Reb and a brother who was out fighting them, you might understand. But since you don't, you can live in some fantasy world, pretending like nothing is happening." Verly jabbed her needle in and out, in and out as she talked. "But I know there's a war on. Just living here and having to work hard every day reminds me of the truth. And I wouldn't be caught dead playing with someone who fraternizes with the enemy!"

It was a good thing Elise was holding the porch railing, or she might have tumbled down. Her knees felt like jelly. "If that's the way you feel, I guess I'll leave."

"Please do, and be quick about it."

Elise mounted Dusty, giving the horse a gentle pat on the side as she did so. Sadly, she rode home.

As the long summer wore on, Elise spent more and more time at Milt's cabin. He was hobbling around a bit better each day. He referred to her and Samuel as two "angels of mercy," saying God sent them to him at exactly the moment he'd prayed.

He showed Elise daguerreotypes of his wife and son when their family was together and happy. "I tried my best to talk Simon out of siding with his ma's people," Milt told her one day. "But young men are so bullheaded. He was determined he would defend her honor by fighting with the Rebels. I'm not all that sure he even knew why they were fighting." He shook his head. "Maybe many of the young boys who die on the battlefields aren't sure why they're there."

"He's a very handsome boy," Elise said, studying the picture. The boy's face had all the gentle features of his mother's—the long straight nose, the generous smiling mouth. It was no wonder he felt he must go to her birthplace and defend her honor.

"He was a good boy. We had two other children who died in childbirth. Simon was all I had after Beth died. After he left, I didn't think things could get any worse. Then word got out that he'd joined the Confederacy, and I found out they very well could get worse. Much worse."

In their visits, Elise learned that Mr. Finney had had a shoemaker's shop downtown before the war, with many connections to the South. He was soon put out of business by angry people who labeled him a traitor. They boycotted his shop.

"I still have all my tools out there in the shed." He waved toward the back. "So if you ever need your shoes repaired, just let me know. I'll be pleased to do it for you for free."

"I'll tell Mama and Papa. I'm sure we have a few shoes you could work on. Especially Peter's. Mama says he wears his shoes out faster than she can purchase new ones."

Since Milt wasn't able to get out, Elise began bringing him a newspaper on each visit. He was so grateful. Even though he had no idea where Simon was—or if his son were still alive—he wanted to know all the war news.

When he read the news that George McClellan was the Democratic candidate for the presidency against Lincoln, Milt just shook his head. "He was inept as a general. What makes them think he'd be any better as a president?"

"His wife, Mary, was a friend of my aunt Ella's. That is, before they moved back east."

"Oh," Milt said, "beg your pardon. I didn't mean to speak poorly of friends of your family."

"That's all right," she assured him. "My papa's said the same thing about McClellan many times. 'A good organizer,' he'd say, 'but a poor fighter.'"

"That's about the size of it," Milt replied.

One day when she brought the paper, they read together about Admiral Farragut winning the Battle of Mobile Bay for the Union.

"That's just what Lincoln needs right now," Milt said. "This victory will help him win the candidacy."

"Do you think Mr. Lincoln will be reelected?" Elise asked. So many people whom she'd heard talking about it were divided in their thinking.

But Milt quickly said, "Yes, I do. Even those who are opposed to him know he's the only one who can bring us through this mess we're in!"

As August drew to a close, Elise dreaded the start of school. During the summer, she saw Verly only on Sundays at church. Verly was careful never to look across the aisle at Elise. She kept her eyes straight ahead, her face expressionless. If that was how she acted once a week, Elise couldn't imagine what she might be like once school started. But she found out soon enough.

When school began in September, Verly quickly told the other children in sixth grade that Elise had befriended a traitor. Some of them had heard of Milton Finney, though Elise was sure they didn't really know him—not like she knew him. The children avoided her, and at recess, no one would play with her.

As she sat in the classroom, Elise remembered when Verly first came to Walnut Hills—how she'd befriended the new girl and introduced her to the other students. She remembered how they'd sat together the previous spring and worked nearly every day on the play. How quickly everything had changed. The anger she felt made her want to lash out at Verly and hurt her somehow.

When Elise came home from the first day of school, Berdeen took one look at her and demanded to know what was wrong. Peter and Samuel had walked to town to help Papa after school, so she'd walked home all by herself.

"It's Verly," Elise said. "She's told everyone that I'm a Southern sympathizer because Mr. Finney is my friend." Suddenly, tears spilled down her cheeks. Tears that had been building up all day.

"There, there, wee lassie." Berdeen came close and wrapped her arms about Elise and held her close. "Your little friend is only speaking out of her own heart full of pain and anger. She canna get at a real Rebel to be angry at for killing her papa, so she's lashing out at the nearest thing she can find."

"But I'm her friend," Elise said between sobs. "I helped her make friends when she first came, and we even wrote the play together."

Berdeen nodded. "It's true, and you know it's true. But she canna see it just now. More's the pity, too, I say." Berdeen dried Elise's tears on her apron. "We'll set ourselves to praying, that's what we'll do. That the good Lord will take the scales off her eyes, and she'll see truth once again."

"But what can I do, Berdeen? She's turned everyone against me. No one wants to play with me."

"You dinna worry your pretty head about that, lassie. The others won't follow her lead for long. They know you too well."

"I hope you're right," Elise said, pulling out her hankie and blowing her nose. "I couldn't stand this for very long."

"Ah, and think for a moment how it is for Mr. Finney—every day and every night. You're tasting just a wee bit of his daily fare."

Elise knew Berdeen was right. "I've never suffered as much as he has. And you know something else, Berdeen?"

"What, luv?"

"I'm very sorry Verly's lost her daddy, but no matter what she says or does, I'll never be sorry I'm Milt's friend."

"That's my girl," Berdeen said, giving her a loving pat. "Do what you know is right, and accept the consequences."

But Elise soon learned accepting the consequences was easier to talk about than to live out.

CHAPTER 10

Dr. Harvey Comes Home

"Mama, I want to quit school," Elise announced one evening in October. She'd come home from another terrible day at school and was surprised to find Mama at home. She'd come home early from helping at the hospital, and it provided the perfect moment for Elise to air her griefs.

"Girls don't need schooling," she went on. "I want to stay home and help you and Berdeen. I can study at home just as well as at school. And even better."

Mama's pretty brows rose, and her dark eyes showed surprise. "Whatever makes you say such a thing? You love school."

Mama had been helping Berdeen in the kitchen, and Berdeen chose this moment to say, "Nay, madam, our lassie *used* to love school. Not anymore!"

Mama pulled Elise to a chair and asked her to sit down as she listened to the story of what Verly was doing at school. Mama shook her head. "I'm sorry you've had to endure this, my little pet. I'll talk to Papa. Perhaps we can arrange something."

Mama glanced over at Berdeen. "The agonies of war," she said to her sadly. "I see them every day etched on the faces of the wounded men and boys. But the tendrils of it reach even into a schoolroom—miles from a battlefield."

"Yes'm. It's the gospel truth, it is!"

Papa was no stranger to persecution. Before the war, he'd been an avid abolitionist, aiding runaway slaves and defending them in court. He knew exactly what it was like to have people say cruel, unjust things. But Papa told Elise the answer wasn't in running away from the problem.

He told her about his experiences in school when he debated against slavery and how one student in particular constantly attacked him and tried to get the other students to do the same thing. "Continue to attend school," Papa said. "Continue to maintain your dignity, and the thing will work itself out."

They were difficult words to swallow. The days stretching out before Elise seemed endless. There was nothing to look forward to. Though the open insults at school gradually stopped, still no one played with her at recess, and no one wanted her for a reading or spelling partner during class. Elise couldn't remember ever feeling so alone. The only bright spots in her life were the interesting visits she had with Milt Finney.

Good news arrived in October—reports of General Philip Sheridan destroying the Shenandoah Valley in Virginia, which in effect cut off the food supply for the Confederate army.

"An army travels on its stomach," Milt told Elise. "No matter how experienced your troops, if you don't have food for them, they're useless. It looks as though the South will have no food." He shook his head, his hazel eyes saddened. "How wretched that it should come to this."

Milt Finney had been right about the Union victories working in President Lincoln's favor. In November, the president was reelected in spite of all the predictions to the contrary. Bells pealed out the joyous news, and people rejoiced in the streets of Cincinnati. Papa called his family together in his library that evening—Berdeen included—and they read scripture and praised God for the miracle.

"Only Abraham Lincoln can bind up the wounds that have so scarred this nation," Papa said to them. "We must be diligent to pray for him every day."

Milt Finney, who was now back on his feet and feeling fit, echoed Papa's remarks. When Elise next visited him, Milt told her that President Lincoln was "a man of love and compassion but full of godly wisdom." Elise knew in her heart that was true.

Since Verly and her mother, Gladys, were such good friends with Aunt Ella and her family, Verly was present at any events that included relatives and guests. Elise found herself dreading the upcoming holidays.

Then one evening only two days before Thanksgiving, Alan drove Aunt Ella over in a buggy to read them a letter from Uncle George. As soon as Aunt Ella entered the house, everyone could see that something was dreadfully wrong. "I've heard from George," she said after she'd taken a seat in one of the parlor chairs. "He's been wounded and is on his way home."

Stunned silence filled the room. Even though Uncle George was behind the lines working in the medical tents, and even though he had a white cloth tied about his arm, he hadn't been safe. Elise could tell her aunt wasn't sure whether to be sad about the injury or glad that her husband was coming home. Aunt Ella read them the letter Uncle George had written, telling how it had happened:

The musket balls were whizzing past us continually, and cannon fire was all about us with deafening explosions. I had

*to shut my mind to their existence. At last one came that I
couldn't ignore. The one that took me down.*

Aunt Ella looked up from reading the letter. "He says so little
about how badly he was wounded, I have no idea what to expect."

"Where is he now?" Mama asked gently.

"The letter was posted from Washington, D.C. He's at a hospital there. He said they will be putting him on a train when he's
able." She gave a shrug. "But I've no idea when that will be."

The years of being without her husband were beginning to tell
on Aunt Ella. Though she was still gracious and lovely, there was
a hint of weariness in her eyes and voice.

"I plan to be at the telegraph office each day until we hear
details of his arrival," Alan told them.

Looking at her tall, rugged cousin, Elise wondered if Uncle
George would even recognize his son.

"Has Melissa heard from Jeremiah recently?" Mama asked.

Aunt Ella nodded. "The letters are shorter. One can tell from
the tone that he has suffered much. I believe all the soldiers are
weary to their very souls of so much fighting."

"It won't be much longer now," Papa put in. "There's no way
the South can continue to hold out."

"I hope you're right," Aunt Ella said as she rose to leave. "As
soon as we receive word of George's arrival, I'll send Alan to let
you know."

A cloud hung over their Thanksgiving celebration. Everyone's
mind was on Uncle George's return. They even talked of postpon-
ing their celebration until he came, but Aunt Ella didn't think that
was best. "He may be spending several days in the hospital when
he arrives," she told them. No one knew what to expect.

Thanksgiving dinner was held at the Brannon home. It was the first gathering that included Charles's wife, Alison, the newest member of their family. Her cheery presence was a blessing for everyone. Elise asked Mama for permission to sit beside Alison at the dinner table. She wanted to stay as far away from Verly as possible. Alison's bright laughter made the day more bearable.

Shortly before Christmas, Dr. George Harvey, chief medical officer in the Union army, returned to Cincinnati. He was a changed man. The first time Elise saw him, she didn't think she could stand it. He was pale and gaunt. His eyes had a strange, faraway look in them. He'd taken a musket ball in his chest, which narrowly missed his heart. He was fortunate to be alive.

He was so ill that he was taken directly from the train to the hospital. Aunt Ella spent nearly every hour at his side. After spending years nursing the sick and wounded at the hospital, now she was tending her own husband.

Each time Elise went with Mama to visit Uncle George, she took a scrap of paper with her on which she'd penned one of her riddles. When no one was looking, she'd slip it beneath his pillow.

One day as they were leaving, Aunt Ella walked with them down the hall a short way. To Mama, she said, "His body is home, Louisa, but his heart is back with his men. He's suffering with guilt for having left them behind. Sometimes when I'm talking with him, it's as though he's not heard a word I said. In the night hours, he's still talking to his aides and calling for help for the wounded."

Mama patted Aunt Ella and said, "It's only been a few days. These things take time. He'll soon be his old self again."

"I pray so, Louisa," Aunt Ella replied. "I pray so."

The day before Christmas, Uncle George was allowed to go home. Aunt Ella told the Brannons she felt they would have their own small Christmas celebration alone. Guests and noise might be too much for the sick man.

Mama and Papa understood. Elise was almost relieved. Even though she loved her cousins, spending Christmas at home meant she wouldn't have to be around Verly and her cold stare.

But things weren't boding well for Uncle George. Though he was thankful to be home with his family, Aunt Ella said he just sat and stared into space. When his family attempted to engage him in conversation, he'd talk for a short time and then forget what he'd been discussing. The twins and Melissa were heartbroken. Aunt Ella was beside herself.

When Elise told Milt about it, he said, "War does funny things to people, Elise. Sometimes it can affect the mind."

She was sitting with him at his kitchen table. As usual, he had several newspapers spread out. He'd been doing a good deal of hunting since cold weather set in, so his larder was full once again. Nevertheless, Elise liked to take him special foods like Berdeen's delicious bread pudding all drizzled with maple syrup.

"But how can a person's mind be fixed?" she asked. "They can operate on the body, but what can be done about the mind?"

Milt shook his head. "Only God knows. We can pray for him. Perhaps in time, being surrounded by his loving family will take care of everything."

"Everyone thought he would return and jump right back into his practice. . . ."

"And take up where he left off?" Milt finished her sentence for her.

"Something like that."

"But that is to deny the horrors he lived with nearly every day for over two years. One cannot easily erase that, Elise. He's no doubt lost count of all the arms and legs he's sawed off and the young boys who've died in his arms."

Elise shivered at the mention of the amputations that she knew took place daily on the battlefields.

"Sorry," he said quickly. "I didn't mean to be quite so graphic."

But she knew Milt was right. They'd been foolish to think everything would be as before. As she rode home that day, she thought about it a great deal. Because of this war that had split their nation, nothing would ever be the same again.

New Year's Eve was even more solemn than the year before. It was as though war was a way of life for the country. January and February were interminably long for Elise. She spent hours in the stables with the horses. She and Chancy worked with Chancellor in the riding arena, getting him accustomed to a light halter. Chancy kept telling her that Chancellor was going to be one of their best horses.

On March 4, President Lincoln was inaugurated for his second term of office. The speech he gave was incredibly short. "Very similar," Papa said, "to the length of his address to the people at Gettysburg."

"A man of his wisdom takes fewer words to make his point," Mama added.

They were sitting together in Papa's library a few days following the inauguration. Papa shared with them the accounts from the newspapers as well as thoughts from letters he received from

Secretary Chase. It was Secretary Chase who had held the Bible on which Mr. Lincoln placed his hand to take the oath.

"Salmon says in his letter that upon taking the oath, Mr. Lincoln leaned down and kissed the Bible," Papa told them. "If we know nothing else of our beloved leader, we know he reveres God's Word."

"I wish we could have been there," Samuel said.

"What did Mr. Lincoln say?" Elise wanted to know. "Tell us about his speech."

"The first of the speech points directly to the atrocities of slavery and how it was localized in the South," Papa said. Then he quoted from the president's speech: " 'These slaves constituted a peculiar and powerful interest. All knew that this interest was somehow the cause of war.' "

Papa looked at them then. "Mr. Lincoln acknowledges that slavery was the fault of both the North and the South. That we have all suffered for the horrible atrocities of that institution." Papa then read the closing remarks: " 'With malice toward none, with charity for all, with firmness in the right as God gives us to see the right, let us strive on to finish the work we are in, to bind up the nation's wounds, to care for him who shall have borne the battle and for his widow and his orphan, to do all which may achieve and cherish a just and lasting peace among ourselves and with all nations.' "

They were all quiet. Then Berdeen said, "It's like the music of a bubbling little brook. Such gentle, kind, and loving words."

"Sounds to me like he wants to forgive the South, Papa," Samuel said. "Is that what you think?"

Papa nodded. "That's exactly what I think. And we're all the better for it. When the war is over—whenever that blessed day may come—you can be assured that President Lincoln's forgiving spirit will allow us to bind up the wounds just as he said."

On a warm day in March, Elise saddled Dusty and went for a long ride out in the country. How she'd missed her long rides through the cold, lonely months of winter. If she had her way, life would be eternally spring with never a cold day.

Outside the city stood rolling hills full of dense forests. For the most part, she remained on the main roads. There'd been rumors of bands of army deserters in the area. Deserters were desperate men, often hungry, sometimes sick and wounded. They traveled in bands to help one another. If they were caught, they could face imprisonment or a firing squad for desertion.

But on this day, Elise nearly ran smack into one such band of men. She'd ridden to a small lake that she enjoyed visiting. As she approached the lake, she heard voices, and her throat burned from the acrid smoke of a campfire. Leaving Dusty tied to a bramble bush, Elise crept forward carefully through the thick underbrush. Peeking through the brush, she saw a camp across the lake.

A group of deserters had pitched their small tents in the clearing, and their voices carried clearly across the still water. Elise wondered how they were finding food at this time of year. There was no grain in the fields and no fruit on the trees. They had to be very hungry. And very cold.

The next afternoon, when no one was about, Elise filled a towsack with apples and sweet potatoes from Berdeen's root cellar. She slung the bag over Dusty's back and returned to the lake up in the hills. She wasn't quite sure how to leave the food so the men could find it and yet not discover her. Finally, she came up with the idea of hanging the towsack from a limb. Any soldier worth his salt would see it hanging there through the gray leafless trees.

The next day at school as Elise watched Verly across the room, she wondered what Verly's reaction would be if she knew Elise gave aid to deserters. She might be even angrier than when she'd learned Elise befriended Milt. Elise kept hoping through the passing months that Verly would have a change of heart. Her face was always sad. It made Elise think of her favorite verse of scripture: "A merry heart doeth good like a medicine, but a broken spirit drieth the bones."

A few of the girls were beginning to talk to Elise once again, and a couple of them asked her to play skip rope at recess. No one was aware of her ongoing friendship with Milt Finney. She didn't tell, and no one asked. It was as though nearly everyone had forgotten about it. One day Elise heard another girl say, "It's no fun to be with Verly Boyd because she never laughs or smiles."

Elise remembered how much the two of them had laughed together as they wrote their play and practiced it. How she would love to hear her old friend laugh that way once again.

CHAPTER 11

Caught by Deserters

Elise wasn't foolish enough to go near the camp of deserters very often. After all, these men were not only desperate, they were soldiers who knew how to keep an eagle eye out. She figured they wouldn't stay long in the area anyway. From what she'd learned from Milt, deserters had to keep on the move for fear of being captured. What a terrible life that must be.

One Saturday she was able to take a loaf of bread and a round of cheese from the pantry. Berdeen was out cultivating her kitchen garden, preparing it for the first plantings. That gave Elise the opportunity to take a few things from the pantry and carrots and turnips from the root cellar, as well.

Again she slung the towsack on her horse and rode out of town to the area where the men were camped. She found herself hoping the camp would be deserted and the men gone, but it wasn't to be. She smelled the fires before she even approached the clearing. This time, she left Dusty farther back so she could quietly move through the brush and hang the sack on the tree.

Suddenly, a voice behind her said, "That's as fur as you'll go, missy."

She gasped and turned about to see a lanky, bearded man pointing a musket right at her. She could feel her heart pounding in her throat, and her mouth went all dry.

"I'll be hornswoggled. Wait'll Duffy hears this," he said. "It's a little bit of a girl what's brung us vittles." He held the musket tight and reached out his hand. "Give me the sack."

Elise slung it toward him, and he picked it up. He waved the musket then. "Head on out thataway. I need to see what Duffy wants me to do with you. He said someone was trying to trap us and that we needed to get goin'."

"My horse—"

"I saw that horse. Purty thing. We'll lead him around with us."

After winding about through the thick brush and trees, they approached the camp. Duffy, she soon learned, was Sergeant Duffield, who acted as leader of the motley group.

"Looka here, Duffy," the man called out. "Here's what brung us them apples. Just a little girl."

Duffy was a lean, leathery young man with the look of premature age in the hardened lines of his face. "I knowed you was a fool, Gettler!" he spatted. "You ain't even thinking. Shoulda left her be and come on back here. We coulda got outta here quick like afore she brings anyone."

Elise glanced around at the men who came up to see this intruder in their camp. Several were wounded, and none looked well. Just then she heard a loud groan coming from one of the tents.

"How's Boyd?" asked Gettler.

Another man squatting at the fire shook his head. "Not good."

Elise could hardly believe her ears. *Boyd. They said the name Boyd.* Could Alexander Boyd be lying ill in that tent? Struggling not to act surprised, she knew she had to do something. But what?

"Sergeant Duffield, my uncle is an army doctor," she said, forcing her voice to be calm. "He came home just before Christmas."

"Don't try no trickery, missy," the sergeant said, his voice cold and gruff. "We don't need nobody, and you ain't sending nobody. We got nothing to lose. We'd just as soon shoot anyone what comes after us."

"I know that," she said, "but you know army doctors are neutral. They have to be. He would understand. . ." She didn't know how to finish the sentence. Uncle George had spent years helping soldier boys just like these.

The man at the fire stood up. His leg was wrapped in bandages, and he limped as he walked. "Seems like she's truthful, Duffy. I say we let her bring a doc out here."

"Me, too," Gettler echoed. "We all need a doc bad."

"I don't!" The sergeant spat out the words.

"But the boy does." Gettler waved toward the tent.

"Whatta the rest of you say?" the sergeant asked.

They all agreed—all except the sergeant—that Elise should be allowed to go and bring back her uncle. Now Elise faced yet another dilemma. How would she ever persuade Uncle George to come?

Gettler brought Dusty up and steadied the horse as he gave Elise a hand up. She was touched by his mannerliness and thanked him kindly.

"Them apples you brung was right tasty. We shore want to thank you."

"I was pleased to do it," she replied. "I'll be back with the doctor soon as I can."

"She'll be back with the law," Duffy said. "Mark my word. No one cares about deserters."

"I do," she said simply.

As Elise rode back to town, she wondered what to do next. She'd promised to bring a doctor, and she would do her very best to keep her word to the men. Over and over she wondered if the boy lying in that tent might be Mrs. Boyd's son and Verly's brother. But there might be scores of soldier boys by the name of Boyd. They hadn't said his first name. She could only wait and see. One thing at a time.

When Elise rode up to the Harvey boardinghouse, Verly was outside. Seeing Elise approaching, Verly quickly went inside.

Tying Dusty to the hitching post, Elise tripped up the porch steps and knocked. Aunt Ella came to the door.

"Why, Elise. Welcome." She glanced outside as though looking to see whom her niece had come with. It had been many months since Elise had come over to visit alone. "What brings you out today?"

"Excuse me, Aunt Ella. Might I see Uncle George? I mean, would you mind if I visited with him? Just me?"

Aunt Ella smiled. "Why, Elise, I'd be pleased for you to visit with the doctor. He's always adored you so. When he first came back, he kept showing me the little riddles you tucked under his pillow. That was one of the few times I saw him smile."

Elise hadn't known. No one had told her. For all she knew, the riddles had been lost or tossed away.

"I'm glad they helped," she said.

"The doctor is around back in his office. He goes in there most every day, but I'm afraid it's wearing on him. He just sits in there and stares into space."

"Thank you, Aunt Ella." She turned to go back down the porch stairs.

"Bless you, Elise," Aunt Ella called after her.

Around back, Elise knocked gently on the office door. Through the window on the door, she could see Uncle George sitting at his desk. A book was open before him. "Uncle George? It's me, Elise."

"Come in," came the faint reply. "It's open."

She opened the door and went inside. She had many memories of coming in this office as a little girl with a stomachache or earache or some such ailment, and she always left feeling better.

Uncle George looked up from the book in front of him and managed a slight smile. "Welcome, my dear. Did you bring me a new riddle?"

Elise paused a moment and thought.

The doctor leaned back in his chair, and now his eyes appeared to have a little gleam in them. "Come now. Could you ever be without a riddle?"

"I have one. Just give me a minute. Oh yes, I have it. What is it that Adam never saw, never possessed, yet left to each of his children?"

Uncle George looked past her, gazing out the window by the door. Elise didn't know if he was going away in his mind as Aunt Ella said he did so often or if he were really thinking. Suddenly, he answered. "You've got me, Elise. I give up."

"Parents. Adam had no parents."

There was a little hint of a chuckle. "Parents." He shook his head. "I should have thought of that. Parents. Of course." He looked at her. "And to what do I owe the pleasure of this little visit?"

"I've been wondering, now that you're home, will I come to you if I have a stomachache?"

"Are you planning to have a stomachache?"

"No. But what if?"

"Not just yet, Elise. I can't seem to get my mind back onto stomachaches just yet. In fact, I can't seem to get the boys out there off my mind at all." He gave a wave of his hand, which Elise knew indicated the battlefields he'd left behind. "I feel I've deserted them. It's as though I hear them calling to me."

"What if there were soldiers here who needed your help?"

Uncle George shook his head. "You mean the hospital. No, Elise. Your aunt Ella's talked to me about that almost daily. But they have plenty of good doctors at the hospital. They don't need me there."

"I'm not talking about the hospital. I know where there's a group of soldiers. Some are hurt, one's sick real bad, and they have no one!"

Uncle George leaned forward, looking at her with new intensity. "Where, Elise? Where are these men?"

"About a half hour out of town north. In the hills. Deserters. I told them I'd bring a doctor. Would you come?"

"Can the buggy get through up there?"

Elise shook her head. "Not all the way. The underbrush is pretty thick. Horseback would be better."

Uncle George stood to his feet. "I don't have my bag ready."

"You can get it ready." She felt excitement building inside her. "It won't take you long. I'll saddle Sierra for you."

"I'll go tell your aunt."

Elise rested her hand on her uncle's arm. "I wish you wouldn't. I promised to keep their presence a secret."

He nodded. "They're desperate, I know. I'll just tell her that I decided to go for a ride in the country."

"Good."

Within a few moments, they were riding out of town, side by side. Elise was sure Aunt Ella saw Uncle George's bag fastened behind him—but that would only tend to encourage her heart. And her aunt was far too wise to intrude with needless questions!

As they rode along, Uncle George thanked Elise for her many letters while he was away. "I looked forward to every one," he told her. "Your jokes and riddles and drawings became a bright spot to me."

"I'm pleased to know I helped just a little."

"More than a little. Why, the boys started asking me if I'd heard from my niece with the riddles. They were all waiting for new riddles to arrive."

Elise thought about that. It had never occurred to her that her uncle might share her riddles. She tried to picture the men coming to ask about the riddles, the smiles on their faces as they shared them around the campfires. She liked the scene her mind created.

As they turned off the road onto the smaller trail, Elise said, "Don't be surprised if we're met with a loaded musket."

"Be assured, it won't be the first time," he said. Then he told her about the time they'd set up the camp hospital in an abandoned house. Rebels came in, pointed their guns at him, and demanded he treat one of their men.

"What did you do?"

"I told them I would have treated him whether they held a gun to me or not. I removed a musket ball from his leg, and they left."

"You helped a Rebel soldier?"

Uncle George nodded. "It wasn't the first time nor the last."

Elise wondered what Verly would have to say about that. Thinking of Verly made her suddenly remember. "Uncle George, there's a soldier up at that camp by the name of Boyd. I heard them say his name, and they said he was real sick. It could be Mrs. Boyd's son, Alexander. They haven't heard from him for a long time."

Uncle George was quiet again. Elise wondered if she'd lost

him. Perhaps this was too much for him to handle right now. Perhaps she'd been too hasty to call on him.

After a moment, he said, "It's a good chance it's him. When a family doesn't hear from a soldier for a long time, he's either dead or deserted. The first of which means the family will usually receive an official notification letter. Even the ones who are hurt the worst can dictate letters to the nurses and volunteers."

His words made a shiver run up Elise's back.

As they came down to the edge of the lake, Gettler popped up from a bush. "Stop right there. Are ye armed?"

"I'm Dr. George Harvey," Uncle George called out, "chief medical officer for the Fifty-Fourth Ohio Volunteers."

Gettler came forward. He dropped all caution, lowered his musket, and reached out to shake Uncle George's hand. "Glad to meet you, Doc. I'm Private James Gettler. Leastwise I was a private. I ain't sure what I am now. Foller me. I'll take you around to camp."

Duffy wasn't quite as trusting as Gettler, but even he seemed relieved to have help arrive. As Uncle George dismounted, Gettler introduced him to Sergeant Duffield. Then Uncle George said, "I understand a boy here is ill."

Duffy waved toward one of the tents. "He's just a kid."

"Most of them are," Uncle George said. He untied his bag from Sierra and ducked as he entered the tent.

Gettler came over to Elise. "Shore don't know how to thank ye, little missy. That bread and cheese was mighty tasty."

"I'm pleased to help," she answered.

Just then, Uncle George came out from the tent. "Elise," he said, "could you come here?"

Elise knew she had no stomach for sickbeds or sick people in them. She hoped he wasn't expecting her help. When she came to his side, he said, "This *is* Alexander Boyd, Elise. He's inconsolable. He knows he's going to die, and he's begging to see his mother and sister."

CHAPTER 12

Sad Reunion

The reality of her uncle's words hit Elise hard. She knew how desperately Mrs. Boyd had waited for word of her son during the past months. And now here he was, only a few miles away from her, dying. Hot tears burned Elise's eyes. "What can we do?"

"Come and talk to him for a moment. Then we'll see about talking reason to these men."

Everything inside Elise wanted to run away. She forced herself to follow her uncle inside the small tent. On a pallet on the ground lay a handsome young man. The dark hair lying across his forehead made his face seem even paler than it was.

Uncle George motioned her to go to the boy. "Hello, Alexander," she said, kneeling down beside him. "I'm Elise Brannon. I'm friends with your mother and sister. They live in my aunt's boardinghouse." She motioned to Uncle George. "In Uncle George's house, actually."

Alexander managed a smile. "You wrote the play," he said with effort.

"Yes. Verly and I wrote a funny play and put it on."

"She wrote me about it." He coughed a little then. "I didn't want Mama to know I was here. Didn't want her to know I ran scared, but now I don't care. I'm gonna die anyhow. But I'd sure like to see her and little Verly." He reached out his hand and took hold of Elise's arm. "Bring them here, will you? Please?"

The look in his eyes broke her heart. "I'll get them both here. I promise."

His hand dropped. "Thank you," he whispered. "Thank you." Then he said weakly, "Tell Mama I'm real sorry."

When they were back outside the tent, Uncle George said, "Thank you, Elise. The boy needs something to help him hang on until they get here."

"But the sergeant won't let us bring anyone. What'll we do?"

"Leave that to me."

Elise watched as Uncle George talked to the men. He almost seemed like his old self again. Using his gentle persuasion and promising to stay with them through the night, he convinced them to let Elise go back to town to fetch Mrs. Boyd and Verly.

Duffy at first was dead set against it, but the others countered him. "We can skedaddle right out of here, soon as the wimmenfolk are gone," Gettler said. "I feel bad enough beings I'm a deserter. But I'd feel a might sight worse iffen I didn't let that boy see his own mama when she's so close."

Elise was relieved when they finally agreed, but she was greatly disturbed that she should be the one to bear the awful news. She had been so sure it would be Uncle George who would tell the Boyds about Alexander.

As Elise mounted Dusty, Uncle George said to her, "Tell Mrs. Boyd to rent a buggy at the livery stable and come as quickly as possible."

"A buggy can get through iffen she comes in thataway." Gettler pointed out away from the lake in a westerly direction. "When I hear you comin', I'll go up to the road to direct you."

Elise nodded. "I'll hurry."

As Elise turned her horse to head out, Duffy spoke up. "Don't think about double-crossing us, little girl. Or you'll be mighty sorry."

"I have no plan to," she assured him.

All the way back into town, Elise rehearsed how she would tell Mrs. Boyd the news, but she could think of no easy way to tell her. When Elise approached the house, Verly was on the front porch with sewing in her lap. As soon as she saw Elise, Verly got up to disappear into the house.

"Verly," Elise called out, riding Dusty right up to the porch, "don't go."

"I don't care to stay in the presence of the likes of you," she snapped.

"Verly, go get your mama, quickly. It's an emergency!"

"Well," Verly huffed, "what if she doesn't want to talk to you?"

Elise let out a deep sigh. As calmly as she could, she said, "It's time to put down your anger, Verly. This has to do with Alexander."

Verly's blue eyes narrowed. "Are you playing a trick on me?"

"It's no trick. Please hurry."

Verly dropped her sewing in the chair and ran inside. Soon Mrs. Boyd came out the front door, ashen-faced. "What is it, Elise? What about Alexander?"

"Dr. Harvey is with him right now. He's with a band of deserters. . . ."

Mrs. Boyd grabbed the porch post to steady herself. "No!"

"You're lying!" Verly said. "Alexander wouldn't."

"Verly, hush," her mother said sharply.

"Alexander's gravely ill. Dr. Harvey says you're to rent a buggy and come quickly. Quickly," she repeated. "The fastest way is for you to ride behind me to the livery."

"I'll get my cloak and bag."

"I'm coming, too," Verly said.

"We can come back and get you," Elise said.

When Mrs. Boyd came back out, Aunt Ella followed. "Your uncle is helping a band of deserters?" she asked Elise.

"That's right, Aunt Ella. But please keep it quiet. They're frightened, desperate men."

"Bless you, Elise," Aunt Ella told her. "You seem to be helping a number of people these days."

Mrs. Boyd wasn't accustomed to riding, but Elise brought Dusty close to the porch. With Aunt Ella's assistance, Mrs. Boyd was able to mount behind Elise.

"Ella," said Mrs. Boyd, "could you have food ready when we come back for Verly?"

"Of course. Come on, Verly." Aunt Ella put her arm around Verly as they went back inside.

In less than an hour, Mrs. Boyd was driving a buggy out of town, following Elise's lead on Dusty. Verly had said not a word. Elise's heart ached for the girl. What a terrible blow this must be for her.

Gettler was standing at the road when they came to the turnoff. He waved his musket for them to stop. "Sorry lady, but I gotta search your buggy."

"We've nothing but food for your men," Mrs. Boyd told him.

His eyes lit up. "I shorely thank you, ma'am, but Duffy still says I gotta look around."

"Please, can't you search it when we get there?" Mrs. Boyd fought back tears, her voice desperate.

Gettler softened. "Guess you ain't planning to harm nothin'." He stepped up to the buggy. "Allow me to drive you around, ma'am. Be faster that way." Mrs. Boyd scooted over, and Gettler jumped up and took the reins.

"I'll meet you at the camp," Elise called out. She turned Dusty off the road onto the trail, hoping against hope that Alexander was still alive.

Duffy saw her coming and reached for his musket. "Where's Gettler?"

"He offered to drive the buggy for Mrs. Boyd. They're coming around by the road." She slid down to the ground. "Is Alexander. . . ?"

"Barely alive. The boy seems to be hanging on in desperation. Your uncle's with him."

Another soldier, barely a boy, came up to her. "We thank you for bringing the doc up here," he said shyly. "My leg's a whole bunch better now that he's fixed it."

Elise smiled at him. "Dr. Harvey needed you boys almost as much as you needed him."

"Now how can that be true?"

"It just is, that's all."

Duffy stiffened as the crunching of the buggy wheels sounded in the distance. "I hope that fool Gettler searched that buggy," he muttered under his breath.

"Did you want him to inventory the food Mrs. Boyd brought with her?" Elise asked him.

Several of the men snickered, and Duffy said no more.

The moment the buggy pulled up and stopped, Verly and her mother stepped down. "Where is he?" Mrs. Boyd asked. "Where's my boy?"

"He's here," Elise said, pointing out the tent where Alexander lay ill. "Uncle George's with him now."

As she said the words, Uncle George appeared at the entrance. "He's been asking for you," he said to Mrs. Boyd. Stepping out of the way, he motioned for the mother and sister to go inside. Then he came to Elise's side and put his arm about her shoulder. "You got them here just in time."

Elise turned and buried her face against Uncle George and wept. He patted her gently in an effort to comfort her. "It's all right," he said. "Even after seeing so many thousands die, I still never grow used to it."

The other soldiers stood about awkwardly, as though they weren't quite sure what they should be doing. "Boyd was a good boy," Gettler said. "He wasn't too keen on cutting out when we did, but we talked him into it. Then he fell sick along the way. I been feeling sorta bad about the whole mess."

Gettler couldn't have been more than twenty-five or so, but he seemed older than the rest. He was squatting near the fire, staring into it. "Two other boys with us died along the way. It's a rough way to travel—running scared."

Uncle George looked down at Elise. "What do you say we take a look at what's packed in that buggy?"

Elise dried her eyes on her handkerchief and nodded in agreement. They brought out two hams, which made the soldier boys sit up and take notice. A towsack was filled with sweet potatoes, apples, and turnips, and a basket held a side of bacon and a dozen or so eggs.

"Iffen we'd had this fare earlier," one of the men said, "ol' Boyd there mightn't have fell sick."

"Fer sure," echoed another.

Suddenly, from the tent came a deep, wailing sob, and Elise knew. Young Alexander Boyd was dead.

"They'll need you now," Uncle George said to her.

"Me? What can I do?"

"You go in there and hug them and cry with them. That's

what's needed at this moment."

Everything inside of Elise fought against it. The grief was too heavy. Too much.

Again, Uncle George's arm was around her shoulder. "Jokes and humorous plays are blessings, Elise, but then the time comes when we weep with those who weep. Just as Jesus bore our griefs, we reach out and help others to bear their grief."

Elise couldn't see that she would be of any use. But she forced herself to obey Uncle George. She made that long walk from the buggy to the tent. Verly and her mother were kneeling beside Alexander's still form, leaning on one another and weeping. Elise went over and put her arms around them. Then she wept.

CHAPTER 13

Alexander's Funeral

Shadows stretched long fingers across the clearing, and a cool breeze swept off the lake. Elise felt weariness deep into her bones. It had been an incredibly long day. They were sitting around the fire. The men had fried slices of ham in a skillet and baked the sweet potatoes in the hot coals. They offered tin plates of food to their guests. Elise managed to eat a little, but neither Mrs. Boyd nor Verly had any appetite.

At first, Mrs. Boyd insisted that she remain by Alexander's side through the night, but Uncle George advised against it. "The air will grow quite cold tonight," he told her. "There's nothing you can do for Alexander here. You must go into town and make arrangements. Ask Alan to assist you in hiring a buckboard to transport the coffin. I'll stay here at camp to make sure his body is safe. I'm used to this."

Uncle George glanced around at the men. "I have an idea the soldiers will break camp and move on now."

Duffy nodded. "We got no choice," he said. "We'll leave at daybreak."

"Let me drive the buggy back for you," Elise offered. "I can tie Dusty on behind."

"Thank you, Elise." Mrs. Boyd reached out to clasp Elise's hand. "You've done so much. If it hadn't been for you, Verly and I would never have been able to say good-bye to Alexander." She began to weep again. Verly remained ashen-faced and still.

When the Boyds and Elise were settled in the buggy, Gettler came up to Elise. "Can you find your way out?"

Elise nodded. "I know the way."

"Yer a right perky little thing. Hope someday I'll have a young'un just like you."

The kind words made her smile. "Thank you, Gettler. I'll be praying for your safety. For all of you."

"I'm much obliged."

Dusk was gathering as Elise drove the buggy away from the lake and onto the main road. Uncle George had lit the lanterns on the buggy, and the pale golden light shone down the road ahead. Elise made no attempts at conversation for fear of saying something wrong. Mrs. Boyd had gotten control of herself, but Verly continued to sniff and make whimpering sounds into her handkerchief.

They hadn't gone far when suddenly a horse came out of the underbrush onto the road. Elise pulled back on the reins. Then with relief she recognized Milt.

"Elise Brannon," he said. "What're you doing out and about at this time of night?" He shaded his eyes against the lantern glare. "And other ladies with you? What's your papa thinking of? Doesn't he know there're bands of deserters in the area?"

"Oh, Milt, we just came from a camp of deserters. This is Mrs. Gladys Boyd and her daughter, Verly. Mrs. Boyd's son was with the band."

"My boy was ill," Mrs. Boyd said, "but because of Elise here, we were able to be with him before his homecoming." She dabbed at her eyes with her hankie. "You must be Milton Finney. I've heard Elise speak of you."

"That I am." Milt rode up next to the buggy. "And please accept my deepest consolation on the death of your son, ma'am. I hope you know that just because he was with deserters doesn't mean he was a coward. Many men both old and young have walked away from the fighting by the hundreds, not so much due to fear, but due to a weariness of all the killing."

"Thank you for saying so," Mrs. Boyd replied. "Your kind words are a blessing at a moment like this."

"I'll ride along with you for a ways," he said. "At least until you get to the edge of town."

"Thanks, Milt," Elise said. "That would make all of us feel better."

"Excuse me, ma'am, if I might be so forward, but have you plans for your son's coffin?"

The words brought a little sob from Mrs. Boyd, and she turned her head away. Elise rubbed her fingers together in a sign of money so only Milt could see and shook her head. She and Uncle George had already discussed Mrs. Boyd's dire financial situation, wondering how they could help her purchase a coffin for her son without offending her pride.

Milt caught Elise's meaning instantly. "Sorry if I caused you anguish, ma'am, but I'm a right fair carpenter, and I have plenty of lumber. I'd like to offer my services if you would allow me. Your son will have as fine a coffin as can be purchased and at no cost to you."

Mrs. Boyd looked over at Milt, and Elise could see a glint of hope in her eyes. "I'm not accustomed to receiving gifts from strangers," she said, "but it does sound like an answer to prayer."

"I'm not a stranger at all, but a friend of a friend." He made a little wave to Elise.

"Yes, yes," Mrs. Boyd answered. "So you are."

"I'll work through the night and have it done by midday tomorrow."

When they reached the edge of town, Milt tipped his hat. "This is where I'll leave you." To Elise, he said, "By the way, those boys up there at the camp, have they heard of Mr. Lincoln's amnesty plan for deserters?"

"Amnesty plan?" Mrs. Boyd repeated. "There's amnesty for the deserters?"

"Yes, ma'am, there is."

Mrs. Boyd looked at Elise. "Did you know?"

Elise shook her head. "Even Uncle George didn't know."

"All they have to do is report to the nearest recruiting office, and they'll be offered work camps till the end of the war. They need have no fear of prison." Milt turned his horse to leave. "I'll go back and tell them. Then I'll get to work on that coffin. See you tomorrow."

"See you, Milt," Elise called out. "And thank you."

As they rode down Montgomery Road toward Walnut Hills, Mrs. Boyd said, "If only the men had known, Alexander might still be alive."

"You can't know that," Elise said. "Papa always says no use speculating on the past unless you aim to learn from it."

"That's true," Mrs. Boyd agreed. "I should be very thankful. How many thousands of mothers have lost sons in this war and were never able to say good-bye. And so many of them were unable to provide even a coffin for their boys' bodies."

Elise didn't know what to say, so she kept quiet and concentrated on driving the buggy.

"What a gentle and caring man Mr. Finney is," Mrs. Boyd reflected. "And so free of malice. I can't believe he's the man I've heard so many terrible things about."

Elise could have said, "I told you so." Instead she said, "Your description of him is so true." She carefully didn't look at Verly.

Aunt Ella had gotten word to Mama and Papa of Elise's whereabouts. When Elise finally got home, both parents were relieved to see her. Berdeen had hot potato soup on the stove, and Elise downed two bowls. The family was gathered in the kitchen, sitting at the table with her, firing questions in volleys.

"Weren't you scared being with those deserters?" Peter wanted to know. She assured him she was not.

"How did you convince Dr. Harvey to accompany you?" Mama asked.

"And how did he act?" Papa put in. "Was he clear-headed? Your aunt Ella's been so concerned about him."

So Elise told them the story from the beginning, in as much detail as her tired body and mind would allow. When she came to the part about the amnesty, Papa said, "Many people were upset when the president put that plan into action."

"It's so like our forgiving president," Mama added. "Think of the young men it will help."

"But," put in Samuel, "think of the men roaming around the countryside, not knowing. They stay away from towns so as not to be caught, so they aren't aware they've been forgiven."

Elise nodded as she remembered Duffy, Gettler, and the others. They were in such a sad condition—cold, weary, footsore, and hungry. They would be overjoyed at Milt's news.

When she told of how Milt met them along the way, Mama smiled. "Sooner or later that man will receive his reinstatement to society. He's been treated so cruelly, and yet he's maintained his dignity."

"Mama, Papa," Elise said, "may he go with us to Alexander's funeral? I mean ride right in our carriage? It would show folks that we believe in him." Elise's papa was respected in the city, and his vote of confidence might make a difference in how people treated Milt.

"You invite him, Elise," Papa said. "If he accepts, I will be proud to have him ride with us."

Gladys Boyd had become well known in the community during the years since her husband had marched off to war. Her excellent seamstress skills had put her in touch with a wide variety of people. In addition, her friendship with Ella Harvey had widened her circle of friends. Therefore, her son's funeral was attended by a large group of people.

To her credit, Mrs. Boyd never tried to hide the fact that Alexander was a deserter. She held her head high and managed to conduct herself with dignity. Close by her side, Verly was having a difficult time. From where Elise sat in the church, she could tell Verly was hurt. Surely she must feel more alone than ever.

Milt had accepted Papa's invitation, and he was sitting in the pew with them, right between Samuel and Papa. Even Peter took a liking to the big man.

Papa made sure Alexander Boyd received full military honors, with a volunteer militia company standing at attention outside the church. Papa said, "The boy might have died not knowing he was forgiven, but we know and will act accordingly."

Mrs. Boyd was deeply grateful and voiced her thanks many

times to Papa, Uncle George, and Milt for all their help.

Following the funeral, the drums rolled and fifes played as the coffin was borne on a horse-drawn cart to the graveyard. The mourners followed on foot.

Mrs. Boyd and Verly wept as the coffin was lowered into the freshly dug grave. A bugle sounded taps, and the melancholy notes floated on the early spring air and reminded each of them of the thousands of others who had died because of the long war.

When the burial service was over, people broke up into tight little knots in the grassy area, talking softly among themselves. Elise felt someone touch her arm. It was a red-eyed Verly.

"Oh, Elise, I was such a fool—blind and full of bitterness. I'm so sorry for the way I acted toward you. I called you a traitor when all the time my own brother was a deserter. Can you ever find it in your heart to forgive me?"

Elise flung her arms about her friend. Through her tears, she said, "I forgave you long ago, Verly. Just like with Mr. Lincoln's amnesty, sometimes it takes awhile for the news to catch up."

"I'm grateful to see you two becoming friends once again," Mama said with a smile.

"Look there," Peter said, pointing. "Mr. Finney is making a friend, too—it's Mrs. Boyd."

Elise looked to where Peter pointed. Sure enough, the two were talking together in the shade of a towering oak tree. In spite of her black widow's garments and her saddened countenance, Verly's mother looked quite attractive.

"They make a handsome couple," Papa said.

Verly smiled. "Right handsome," she agreed. "Right handsome."

CHAPTER 14

Verly's New Family

The boardinghouse sign had been taken down the very day Dr. Harvey arrived back in the city. But the sign that read GEORGE HARVEY, MEDICAL DOCTOR was still stored in the back of the family carriage house. The week after Uncle George helped the deserters in their camp, Aunt Ella told Mama that he went to the carriage house himself and retrieved his business sign.

He scrubbed the old sign, touched up the paint, and hung it on the hinges in the wrought-iron frame out front. Aunt Ella also told Mama that he seemed more like himself with every passing day. The patients who'd known and loved him in the years before the war slowly but surely began to come by the office again to see their doctor.

Melissa at long last received word of her husband, Jeremiah Baird. He was recovering in a hospital near Washington, D.C. He'd lost a leg, his letter said, but he was all right otherwise. His letter was cheery as he wrote:

> They'll be fitting me with a cork leg here in a few days. That means if I ever tumble into the Ohio River, I'll float to safety and perhaps even carry a few folks along with me.

Later in the letter, he added:

My dearest Melissa, just think of the money we'll save on shoes and stockings, seeing as how I'll only need half as many.

The family was overjoyed not only that Jeremiah was alive, but that his sense of humor was intact. The entire Harvey household was in an uproar as they prepared for Jeremiah's homecoming.

School was fun again now that Elise and Verly played together every recess. The mood of all the students seemed to have changed for the better. Everyone was certain the end of the war had to be very near. The war map that Mrs. Myers followed closely now showed Sherman's march across the Carolinas.

Elise studied the map and wondered how the South could hold out much longer. So much of their food and ammunition supplies had been cut off. How could they be so desperate to continue fighting? Why should any more lives be lost?

Just as Miss Earles had done in fifth grade, Mrs. Myers had created a list of soldiers—friends and relatives of the students in the sixth-grade classroom. Each morning the students prayed for their safety and well-being, and they prayed for the long war to be over.

One day when Elise was visiting Milt, he said he had a favor to ask of her. From a shelf, he took down a nice bowler hat. Bringing it to the table where she was sitting, he handed it to her and said, "Might I ask you to take this to the hatters to be steamed and shaped? It's been sitting for a number of years now, and it's in pretty bad shape."

Elise looked at her friend. "Many people saw you at Alexander's funeral, Milt. No one was unkind to you then. I think you should go to the hatters yourself and see what happens."

He smiled and sat down at the table opposite her. "I had an idea you might say that." Raking his fingers through his dark, thick hair, he said, "That'll take some doing."

"You've come this far. By the way, what's the need of a spiffy hat anyway? Are you going calling?" she teased.

Milt's face colored a bit and he smiled. "I've thought on it. And *that* will take even more courage!"

"But you can do it." She folded up the newspapers they'd been reading together. "It's probably time to unlock your shop again, as well. I mean, you'll need an income if you're thinking of courting."

"Elise Brannon, you are the most candid child I've ever had the pleasure to meet."

"Is that a compliment?"

"Very much a compliment."

"Well?"

"Well, what?"

"When are you going to unlock the shop? How about today? We could pack up your tools and carry them down there today. I can help you clean up and straighten things."

Milt didn't take her bait right away. "It's not as easy as that, I'm afraid. Things have changed. During the war, factories turned out shoes for the soldiers by the hundreds, Elise. I'm not sure there'll be any market for custom-made shoes anymore. Everything is being manufactured these days."

"But people will always need their factory-made shoes repaired. And there'll always be the few who prefer your custom-made shoes." She paused. "The truth is, you'll never know unless you try."

"Well," he said, grinning, "I can't just sit up here all alone in this cabin, can I?"

"You could—but I don't think you really want to."

Milton Finney slapped both hands on the table, making Elise jump. "No, I don't. I don't want to sit here anymore. Come on,

Elise, let's load up those tools."

All Milt needed to know was whether his old customers would return to him. Elise solicited all their friends and neighbors to take their shoes to his shop. Soon his business was moving forward once again. Only then did he come calling at the Harvey home to see Gladys Boyd.

Verly was all smiles as she told Elise about it at recess the next day. "He wore a fine suit and a trim bowler hat," she said excitedly. "He came riding up looking like a real gentleman."

"He *is* a real gentleman," Elise put in.

"Then he knocked at the door, and when Mrs. Harvey answered, he told her he'd come calling for Mrs. Boyd and could he speak to her in the parlor."

"And did your mama come down?"

"She did, but you should have seen her flying about our room, worrying about her hair, pinching her cheeks to pink them up a little, then changing quickly into a fresh dress. I wanted to laugh right out loud. She acted as though she were Alicia's age."

"Perhaps she felt that way, as well." The bell was ringing for recess to be over, but Elise hurriedly asked, "So what happened next?"

"What do you think? He's asked for Mama's hand in marriage!"

"Oh, Verly." Elise hugged her friend, and they squealed with delight until Mrs. Myers hushed them.

As they lined up in straight rows with the other students to go in, Verly turned around to Elise and whispered, "I'm going to be in the wedding. Mama's asked that I stand up with her!"

The Harveys insisted the wedding be held in their parlor. It was a small affair, but there was no lack of excitement. The joy of the day was made doubly so by the presence of Lieutenant Jeremiah Baird. Just as with Uncle George, Jeremiah had aged through the years of relentless battles. But his face was wreathed in a smile, and Elise heard him say how thankful he was to be safely home once again. Melissa sat close by his side and held his arm as though she never wanted to release him again.

The date was April 8. Elise felt it was a perfect time for a wedding, being so close to Easter. What promise and hope it represented. She hadn't been this happy for a very long time.

Milt had rented a small cottage. Though he had told his bride that she needn't continue her hard work as a seamstress, she informed all her customers she'd still be available to them. Elise knew Mrs. Boyd would continue to work for a time until Milt could make his way with the shoe shop.

Verly was to stay with the Brannons for a few days so the newly wedded couple could have time alone. That suited Elise and Verly just fine. In fact, it turned out to be perfect.

The girls were just leaving church when a messenger came flying down the street on his horse. "The telegraph lines have been singing all morning," he yelled out to them. Then he whooped and shouted, "The war is over! The war is over!" Sure enough, Lee had surrendered to Grant at Appomattox Courthouse, Virginia.

Suddenly everyone was crying, laughing, shouting, hugging, and whooping about. No one could stand still. No one could contain the infectious hilarity. Grown men had tears streaming down their faces as they smiled and laughed. Bells began their joyous pealing all across the city.

"Come quickly," Papa said. "Let's go downtown!"

They piled quickly into the carriage and joined the throng on Fifth Street. Elise had never seen such a spontaneous gathering.

From out of nowhere, the Volunteer Militia appeared in uniform with their fifes, drums, and bugles. Bands were assembled. Music filled the air. Elise and Verly laughed and laughed as they watched people actually dancing in the streets. At the landing, cannons were shot and explosions filled the air. Soon after, echoes came from similar firings across the Ohio River at Newport Barracks and Covington. Rifles were fired into the air, and the fire bells and church bells never stopped ringing. Hour after hour, the celebration raged on at a fevered pitch.

At intervals, another message would come over the telegraph and send the crowds into another round of cheering and shouting. One such message said that following President Lincoln's remarks made from the balcony of the White House, he called for the navy band to play a rousing chorus of "Dixie."

"We fairly captured it yesterday," the president was reported as saying, "and the attorney general gave me his legal opinion that it is now our property."

As soon as that message was read, the bands on the streets of Cincinnati began to play "Dixie." This brought on yet another frenzy of jubilant cheering. Sometimes a person would just stop and say, "It's over. It's truly over." Hearing the words aloud helped to make it more real.

Several ministers of local churches gathered together and mounted the courthouse stairs. Waving the crowd to silence, they each offered up prayers of thanksgiving to God. One pastor reminded the crowd that the next Thursday would mark the fourth anniversary of the attack on Fort Sumter.

There was no school on Monday. The school superintendent said none of the children would be able to concentrate anyway. That gave Elise and Verly a full day for playing in the spring sunshine.

Everything seemed so perfect. Almost storybook perfect.

They played with Chancellor in the grassy pasture and picnicked in the orchard. They had a tea party and read books. But mostly they just talked.

"Because of you," Verly said, "I have a new papa. And now I'll never have to work hour after hour again as I did for the past few years. You're a wonderful friend, Elise."

"And we'll be friends forever," Elise promised. "Come what may."

"Come what may," Verly agreed.

The cottage where the new Finney family settled was close to town, but Verly would finish out the school year at Walnut Hills Elementary.

"Papa says," Verly told her, "that by next school year, we may be living in Walnut Hills. Then we'll be neighbors once again."

Elise was sure Milt would do just as he promised.

The next Saturday morning, Elise was invited to go to Verly's new home and visit. Now Verly had her own neat little room. They hadn't a bed for her yet, but Verly cared not a whit. "I would sleep on a pallet on the floor forever if it meant having our own home again and having my new papa. He's so kind and good, Elise. And I've never seen Mama so happy." After Elise had seen the inside of the cottage, Verly pulled at her hand. "Come and see the little yard in back. The oak tree is a perfect place for a picnic."

And it was. There was enough room for Milt's horse to graze on the grassy areas and a shed for the horse, as well. The girls spread a blanket beneath the giant oak. Just as Verly's mother was bringing out their lunch, the bells began to ring. Elise looked at Verly. They were stunned. What could it be?

Milt came out the back door. He looked troubled.

"What, Papa?" Verly said, her voice sounding strange. "What is it?"

"I'll go find out." He slipped a bridle on the gray speckled horse and started to mount him bareback. As he did, a messenger came by on horseback with the news no one could believe: "Lincoln was assassinated!" he cried. "The president is dead!"

CHAPTER 15

The Giant Has Fallen

Elise felt as though someone had punched her square in the stomach. She sunk to the blanket beside Verly, and both girls burst into tears. "No, no," Elise cried. "It can't be! It just can't be."

Milt put his arms about Verly's mother as she buried her face in his great chest. Her weeping made a muffled sound.

"Let's walk down to the newspaper," Milt suggested, his own eyes tear-filled. "We'll get the story firsthand."

They found a somber group standing outside the newspaper office. Messengers from the telegraph office were running back and forth. Periodically, they received little snatches of news. After a time, the editor of the paper came outside with a dispatch in his hand.

"This is what we have so far," he said loud enough for all to hear. "President Lincoln and his wife attended a play last evening— Friday—at Ford's Theater in Washington, D.C. A young actor named John Wilkes Booth, who knew both the play and the theater well, entered into a box near the president's and shot him at close range. The president was taken to a nearby house, where he died this morning, April 15, 1865, at 7:22."

Murmurs rippled through the crowd as the reality of the news slowly sunk into their minds. Elise looked at the weeping people around her. Could it have been only last Sunday that these same people had been shouting and cheering? This just couldn't be. She felt numb, as though she were not really there. As though she were floating about in the midst of this sobbing, forlorn crowd. After all the long years of fighting and death—how could it have come to this?

Another announcement came then from the editor. "Major Robert Anderson and his party entered Fort Sumter last evening and raised the Union colors."

Robert Anderson was the same man who'd been in command of the fort when it had been taken four years earlier. Had that news come last week or even a day ago, it would have resulted in cheers and clamorous noise. Now it seemed almost trivial.

Elise whispered to Milt, "I—I think I'd best go on home."

"Yes, Elise. You need to be with your family."

As she turned around, Papa was there. And Mama and her brothers—all with reddened eyes and grim faces. Like all the others, they'd come to hear more concrete news. Papa put his arms about Elise and held her close so she could release her own tears.

Later, he purchased several newspapers and gathered his family together and they drove home. As they went, they watched dark clouds begin to form. The sunshine vanished.

Papa looked up at the sky. "The light's gone out," he said softly. "*Our* light has gone out."

The city was in mourning, the state was in mourning, the entire nation was in mourning. No one in all the land was not touched by the grim news. People felt as if they had lost a close relative or a dear, dear friend. Every house in Walnut Hills was hung with black crepe. Even houses in the poorer districts by the landing had little strips of black cloth fastened to the doorposts.

Elise felt at times as though she could not breathe, as though a vise were clamping down on her heart and soul. Sometimes she found herself weeping and was unable to stop. Each day Papa read to them from the papers. Gradually, the details of the carefully planned, premeditated murder were revealed.

"At least now," Papa said one evening, "Mr. Lincoln's harshest critics have been silenced. Only good will be said of him."

"And," Mama added, "at least now the weary man can have rest."

A letter arrived for Papa from Secretary Salmon Chase. It was Chase who had administered the oath of office to Vice President Andrew Johnson on Saturday morning after President Lincoln died. His letter told of the weeping crowds standing about in the cold rain all day Saturday. He wrote:

> *On Pennsylvania Avenue in front of the Executive Mansion were hundreds of people standing weeping in the gray rain. My heart broke for the colored folks who wailed and moaned as though from the very depth of their souls. They had called him "Father Abraham," and they loved him so dearly. Many of them are now wondering what will become of them now that their dear "father" is gone.*

President Lincoln's funeral was held in Washington, D.C., on the Wednesday after Easter. The newspapers reported that the procession was three miles long, that businesses were closed, and that everyone in the nation's capital gathered to mourn their loss.

One evening Papa read about the route that would be taken by the train carrying the president's body back to his home state of Illinois for burial. Papa looked at his family and said, "I would like the five of us to take the train to Springfield. I've wished many times that we'd gone to President Lincoln's inauguration in March so you could have witnessed that historic occasion. I don't want you to miss this one."

"It says here," Mama said, pointing at the paper, "that the train will be coming right through Columbus. That would be so much closer than going all the way to Illinois."

Papa nodded. "I know, Louisa. But the final destination is his home in Springfield. We'll say good-bye to him there."

"What will become of our nation now, Papa?" Samuel asked. Both Samuel and Peter had been so quiet since the news came. Elise knew each of them had been weeping in private.

"God's hand is upon us, Samuel. The same God in whom our president trusted—that same God will bring us through this wretched ordeal, as well. We can only trust in Him."

It rained day after day. Verly said that God was weeping, and Elise agreed with her. Daily, the newspapers described in vivid detail the hundreds of thousands of mourners who stood in long lines in pouring rain to view the president's body. The body lay in state first in Washington, then at New York's City Hall. Some people waited as long as five and six hours to pay their respects to their fallen leader. The numbers were the greatest, the newspapers reported, at night, when common laborers got off work at the shops and factories.

The scene was repeated at every stop. Papa commented, "How they do heap honor on a man who claimed none."

By reading the newspapers, the Brannons followed the progress of the funeral train westward through New York, to New Jersey and Pennsylvania, and then on toward Ohio. The train was covered with flags, bunting, and black crepe draping. One reporter said, "The out-pouring of grief is more intense the farther west we travel."

Since railroad officials were clearing other trains from the tracks so that the funeral train could progress without delay, Papa said the family would have to leave for Springfield before the funeral train arrived in Ohio.

The morning of April 29, the five Brannons, dressed in their Sunday finest, boarded the earliest train out of the Cincinnati, Dayton, & Hamilton railroad station. At any other time, Elise would have been overjoyed to be going on such a trip. Illinois was two whole states away from Ohio. And the family hadn't taken any rides on the train since before the war started. This trip, however, would not be a holiday. It was a sad farewell.

CHAPTER 16

To Springfield

Peter, who was sitting between Mama and Papa, leaned his sleeping head against Mama's shoulder. The rhythmic rocking of the train had lulled him to sleep. Samuel and Elise sat side by side across from them. The ride seemed very long and tedious. Elise's hoops kept creeping up, and the stays in her new corset bit into her sides. She felt mussed and wrinkled. There'd not been a break in the clouds for ever so long. Though it was only a drizzle now, the dense cloud cover caused dusk to come early.

Samuel had been so quiet, it barely seemed like he was beside her at all. Elise knew he was grieving, but she also thought something else was on his mind, as though he were wrestling deeply with some problem.

"Mama," Elise said, "may Samuel and I walk through the car and stand at the end for a time? A little breath of fresh air would be so delightful."

Mama looked at Papa. "Do you think it would be all right?"

Papa nodded. "I see no harm."

Samuel seemed a little reluctant to move, but she gave him a shake. "Come on, Samuel. Let's stretch for a few minutes."

He got up and allowed her to lead the way down the aisle. She opened the door, and they stepped out onto the railed landing, where the brisk breeze cooled her face. Here the clattering of wheels against the tracks was noisier than inside. Samuel took off his hat, took hold of the railing, and leaned his head out as though to take a drink of the air rushing by.

"You've been so quiet," Elise said. "It's not like you to be so quiet. Is something wrong?"

He turned around and looked at her. He was so much taller now. His eyes were much like Mama's, but they were troubled. "No one's been talking much. Or hadn't you noticed?"

"I've noticed that no one feels like talking. But there's something more going on with you. More than the grieving for Mr. Lincoln."

"You seem pretty sure of yourself."

"Tell me I'm wrong."

He turned around so she couldn't see his face. "I have something I need to tell Papa. I don't know how to tell him." The words whipped around him.

"It wouldn't have to do with your plans for law school, would it?" she asked.

He whirled back around. "Elise Brannon! What are you, some kind of mind reader?"

She smiled. "Who has to be a mind reader? Why don't you tell me what's going on in that head of yours."

"Papa's counting on me, Elise. He's been counting on me for a very long time. But now I'm going to have to disappoint him."

"How could you ever be a disappointment to Papa, Samuel?"

"I'm not going to law school. I'm going to medical school. I'm going into medicine."

"When did you finally realize the truth?"

He studied her. "Are trying to tell me you've known?"

She nodded. "Politics is so rough and tumble, and you're so

130

sensitive. I've always known you had a special touch."

"I guess I've known it, too. Especially after setting Milt Finney's broken leg all by myself."

"Is that what helped you make up your mind?"

"That and talking with Uncle George. He's offered to mentor me."

Elise was surprised. "You mean you've talked with Uncle George but not with Papa?"

"I don't know how to tell him."

"Perhaps he's like me," Elise said.

"And how's that?"

"He's just sitting back, wondering when you are going to discover the truth."

"I don't think it'll be that easy."

"When we get to the hotel in Springfield, you take him aside and tell him you want to talk with him alone. Then just tell him. The sooner he knows, the more he can help you."

Samuel considered her words. "Very well." He brightened and stood up a little straighter. "Very well, I will. I'll just tell him right out."

"That's the way Papa would want it."

When their train made a short stop in Indianapolis late that night, the conductor spread the news that John Wilkes Booth was dead. Shot to death by his captors.

Papa shook his head. "I can't ever remember being glad of a man's death before. I believe this is about the closest I've ever come."

Mama gently patted his arm. "Don't fault yourself, Jack. No one can be expected to feel any differently," she said.

Elise wondered how a man could be so heartless and cruel as to kill a kind and gentle man like President Lincoln. Life was so terribly unfair.

By the time they reached Springfield late the next day, Elise felt stiff and sore from sitting for so many long hours. A carriage at the station took them the short distance to the downtown hotel. Intermittent drizzle still dripped from the sodden skies.

Springfield was much smaller than Cincinnati, and Elise thought it not nearly as pretty. As at home, nearly every building was draped with black crepe. Evergreen arches had been created along the route where the funeral procession would pass. A large sign read WITH MALICE TOWARD NONE; WITH CHARITY FOR ALL, quoting from the president's inaugural speech. Elise saw men wearing black armbands. Everyone was quiet and subdued.

After they were settled in their hotel room, Papa took them to eat in the hotel dining room. The hotel was crowded with guests, and the dining room was full, as well. Yet the atmosphere was quiet, almost like church.

The young man who came out from the kitchen to take their order asked, "Come to see the president?"

"Yes, we did," Papa answered. "All the way from Cincinnati."

The boy seemed impressed. "Cincinnati, the Queen City of the West. Well, welcome to President Lincoln's home."

Peter said, "My papa is a lawyer like Salmon Chase was before he became Secretary of the Treasury. We saw the president before he became president."

Again the waiter seemed duly impressed, and Peter appeared proud to have had the opportunity to brag a little. "Want to read the evening news while you're waiting?" The waiter handed them a Springfield newspaper, and Papa thanked him. "You've probably already heard that they killed Booth."

Papa nodded. "We heard it last evening in Indianapolis."

"Good enough for him, I say. I guess he thought he was going to be a hero in the South. Thought he was doing them some sort of favor."

"The South needed President Lincoln desperately," Papa said. "He was the best friend they had in Washington."

"Mr. Lincoln was a forgiving man," Elise put in. "His plan was to forgive all those who started the war and those who fought against us."

The boy nodded. "Now we'll never know, will we? We'll never know how Mr. Lincoln would have put his plans for forgiveness into action. It's a crying shame, that's what it is. A crying shame." The boy turned and went back to the kitchen.

Papa read to them from the paper. It told about vast numbers of people who filed by the coffin in Ohio and Indiana and how hundreds had stood out in fields in the rural areas to see the train pass by. At night, the train passed hundreds of torches and blazing bonfires lit in tribute to President Lincoln. Men stood bareheaded in the cold rain to pay their respects.

"It says here," Papa told them, "that at journey's end, the coffin will have traveled seventeen hundred miles and will have been seen by more than seven million people."

"It's like nothing I've ever heard of before," Mama said, keeping her voice low. "The people loved him so."

Papa explained that the coffin bearing the president was in Chicago at that very moment and would arrive in Springfield the next morning. "Then it will be our turn to pay our respects," he told them.

That evening before they retired, Samuel asked Papa if he

could speak to him alone. Papa said, "Of course, Samuel," just as Elise knew he would.

The two stepped out of the room, and Mama looked at Elise. The voices sounded low and soft out in the hallway.

"What's that about?" Mama asked.

"I believe you'll know shortly." Elise stepped behind the strung-up curtain and changed out of her travel clothes into her soft flannel nightgown. How good it would feel to be in a bed instead of sleeping upright in the railroad car seat.

There was a small cot for Elise, and the boys were to sleep on the floor. She crawled between the bedding and fought to stay awake until Samuel and Papa came back into the room.

When she heard the knob turning, her drooping eyelids flickered open.

"Louisa," Papa said, "Samuel has an interesting bit of news to share with us."

"Oh?" Mama was brushing out her long, black hair, having unfastened her chignon.

"Can I know the news, too?" Peter asked.

"You sure can," Papa said. He sat down on the bed, pulled off his boots, and gave a sigh. "Go ahead, Samuel."

Samuel's face reddened a bit. "I'm not going to law school."

Mama gave a little gasp and almost dropped her hairbrush. "Not going to law school? But that's what you've always said you wanted. To work with your papa and then go into politics."

"I guess I wanted that because all along I thought Papa wanted it."

"But I wanted it for him because that's what I thought he wanted," Papa added. "Now isn't that a fine howdy-do?"

Mama gave a little laugh. "So pray tell us, Samuel. What are your plans?"

"Can't you guess, Mama?" Elise asked from her cot.

"I can," Peter said. "I know how well he took care of me when I hurt my ankle sledding."

"And how he set Mr. Finney's leg," Elise added.

"And how lovingly he's worked with every horse we've ever had," Papa said.

"I've always said he has that touch." Elise felt herself sinking into a gentle sleep. "Now we'll have two doctors in the family."

"I can't think of a better mentor for you than your uncle George," Papa said.

The last thing Elise remembered was seeing Mama and Papa with their arms about Samuel, telling him how proud they were of him and how happy they were for him. Then she fell asleep.

CHAPTER 17

Good-bye, Mr. Lincoln

"Will it ever stop raining?" Peter asked when he first awoke.

"Will God ever stop weeping?" Mama said.

As each member of the family rose, washed, and dressed, the rain slashed heavily against the windows. A quick breakfast was taken in the hotel restaurant, after which they walked together through the rain to the train station. The train was originally scheduled to arrive at six thirty, but the station manager told the waiting crowd that the funeral train had met with delays along the way and was running late.

As the Brannons waited, the crowd continued to swell until they felt pressed from all sides. But it wasn't a boisterous crowd. As in the restaurant, everyone spoke in hushed tones, almost in whispers.

Papa pulled five pennies from his pocket. "I'm going to lay these on the track," he told them. "When the wheel of the funeral train passes over them, it will flatten them. Each of us will have one as a treasure to keep through the years to remember this day. To remember this moment in history."

"Papa," Elise said, "would you please put a sixth penny on the track? Put one there for Verly, as well."

Papa smiled. "That's my Elise. Always thinking of others."

As she watched him place the coins carefully on the shiny wet iron rail, she thought about his remark. At times in the past, she'd felt Papa was too busy and that he never noticed her. But now she felt differently. He did notice her, and she knew he cared about her very deeply.

Her legs grew tired as they waited and waited. Finally, at around nine o'clock, they heard a long, low whistle as the train approached the station. Elise was so close, she could feel the steam rolling out from the sides of the engine as it chugged into the Springfield station. Bells throughout the city began to toll, and drums from a nearby band began to roll in a soft dirge.

A large portrait of the president framed by a wreath of evergreens was placed on the pilot beams of the locomotive. Smaller daguerreotypes were mounted between the high drivers. Evergreen boughs were strewn about the locomotive, along with yards and yards of draped black crepe. Crepe-trimmed Union flags fluttered from the front cowcatcher.

As the train steamed and hissed to a stop, Papa stepped forward and picked up the six pennies. He handed one to each of them. In Elise's palm, he placed two. She felt the warmth of the metal from having been flattened by the weight of the funeral train.

The funeral entourage got off the train, and the procession began. Men took off their hats, and everyone became silent. Solemnly, slowly, the crowd began to inch away from the station, moving down the street toward the state capitol building where Lincoln had served in the House of Representatives many years earlier.

Mama and Elise wore their rubber boots and stood under their parasols, but they were still getting wet from the steady gray rain. At the capitol, a podium had been erected. While the coffin was taken inside and readied, several officials and politicians spoke eloquently about their slain leader.

Between speeches, the bands played solemn hymns such as the "Doxology" and "Mine Eyes Have Seen the Glory." Tears burned in Elise's eyes as she listened to the sad, soft music.

When the speeches were over, the doors of the capitol were opened, and the crowds moved in that direction. By now it was nearly noon, and Elise's stomach was beginning to growl. Breakfast had been eaten many hours ago, but she didn't care. She was going to say good-bye to President Lincoln.

At long last they were inside, and she and Mama closed their parasols and shook the droplets out of their long, full skirts. It was even quieter inside than out. The only sounds were the rustle of hoop skirts and soft footfalls. Even a slight cough from someone in the crowd seemed noisy.

"You may speak a blessing," Mama whispered to her three children. "But remember, this vessel of clay is just an empty shell. Mr. Lincoln is rejoicing in heaven, set free from his heavy burdens."

The coffin was surrounded by mounds of flowers, evergreen wreaths, and drapes of white satin. Elise was near enough that she could actually see the coffin. The rows of people narrowed from the jumbled bunches into a single-file line. Peter was in front of her, Samuel behind her. Mama and Papa were behind Samuel.

As the line moved, Elise could see the thatch of dark hair and the beard for which Mr. Lincoln was so well known. A few more steps and she could see the rugged, angular face. His face held an expression of rest and total peace.

"Bless you, Mr. Lincoln," she heard Peter say, "for setting the captives free."

Now Elise stood right beside the coffin of President Lincoln. "Bless you, Mr. Lincoln," she said, "for extending forgiveness to the deserters and all those who started the war."

Behind her, Samuel whispered, "Blessings on you, Mr. Lincoln, for preserving our nation."

As Elise stepped down from the platform, she was weeping as she had the first day she received the news. Then Mama had her arms around her, holding her and comforting her and grieving along with her.

That afternoon, Secretary Chase came to the hotel where the Brannons were staying and visited with them. He stayed long enough to eat supper with them in the restaurant. He filled them in on many details of the final days of the war, as well as details of the assassination of the president. The next day, as Mr. Lincoln was buried in the Oak Ridge Cemetery, the Brannons stood near the front in the crowd of thousands, right next to Secretary Chase.

Hymns were sung, eulogies were given, sermons were preached, prayers were said. Rich green cedar boughs carpeted the stone floor of the vault. Flowers were placed in precise arrangements. Mourners carried flowers with them and heaped them on the coffin.

At last all the ceremony was finished. An era had ended. Abraham Lincoln was at rest.

CHAPTER 18

Friends Forever

As soon as Elise returned home, she saddled Dusty to ride to the Finney cottage and give Verly the special penny.

When Elise rode up, Verly came running out the front door to meet her. "Oh, Elise, I'm so glad to see you. Welcome home! I have wonderful news to tell you."

Elise jumped to the ground and tied Dusty to the hitching post. "After all the sadness of the past few weeks, good news would be most welcome," she said.

The May sunshine had finally broken through and was drying up the soggy countryside.

"The day after you left for Springfield, Papa received a letter. A special letter."

"From whom?"

"His son, Simon."

Elise looked at her friend. She remembered how intensely Verly hated anyone who fought for the South. "What did the letter say?" she asked.

"Since Papa didn't know if Simon was dead or alive, that was the first great news—he's alive and he's well." Verly's pretty blue eyes were sparkling. "He wants to come home for a visit. Isn't that wonderful?"

"It is absolutely wonderful. Milt must be ecstatic."

"Oh, he is. We all are." Verly plopped down on the steps of the small front porch. Elise sat down beside her. "Just think," she said, "now I have a new older brother as well as a new papa. I have a whole new family! Isn't God good?"

"That He is, Verly. That He is." Elise had never seen her friend so joyful. Just then Elise remembered why she'd hurried over. Reaching into the pocket of her apron, she said, "I've brought you a little gift."

"A gift? For me? How kind of you."

"Hold out your hand."

Verly extended her palm. "This," Elise said, placing the flattened penny in her friend's hand, "is a coin that Papa laid on the track at Springfield. It was flattened by the funeral train of Mr. Abraham Lincoln."

Verly gazed reverently at the coin. "Thank you, Elise. Thank you for caring enough to share your special moment with me."

"Someday, when we are very old and we're surrounded by our grandchildren and our great-grandchildren, we'll have these coins as a memento of this moment in history."

Verly smiled. "And you know what? I bet we'll still be friends after all those years."

Elise laughed and put her arms about her friend to hug her. It felt wonderful to laugh once again. "Verly," she said, "I bet you're right!"

If you enjoyed

Elise
the Actress

be sure to read other

SISTERS IN TIME

books from BARBOUR PUBLISHING

- Perfect for Girls Ages Eight to Twelve

- History and Faith in Intriguing Stories

- Lead Character Overcomes Personal Challenge

- Covers Seventeenth to Twentieth Centuries

- Collectible Series of Titles

6" x 8 ¼" / Paperback / 144 pages / $3.97

AVAILABLE WHEREVER CHRISTIAN BOOKS ARE SOLD